Donuts on Blanch

A NOVEL

Ben Stephenson

This book is a work of fiction. Names, characters, places and incidents are products of the author's imagination or are used fictitiously. Any resemblance to actual events or locales or persons, living or dead, is entirely coincidental.

Acknowledgements

Amanda for pushing me and for believing in me.

Nick for instilling much needed confidence.

Chapter 1

Mr. Ruggles gazed up at the sign with a sense of satisfaction. It was slightly crooked, he realized. He'd have to get it adjusted immediately. A quick glance down at his wristwatch showed that his cashier was late. How can someone be late on their first day, the day of a grand opening no less? Luckily, Mr. Ruggles had played around with the new checkout technology when he first acquired it, so he was more than capable of ringing up his customers, although it was tricky with his small, scaly fingers. Part of him fumed at the utter lack of respect, as well as the thought of playing cashier on his big day. At least the chef had arrived on time. He sighed and said to no one in particular, "I guess I'll be cutting the ribbon and counting the cash. Hopefully there will be a lot of it."

Mr. Ruggles never went by his first name. After all, why should he? He was sophisticated and well-respected in the lizard community. An established businessman, he owned a dry cleaner where the fanciest lizards often brought their evening wear. He also owned a small construction company specializing in building bungalows for lizards looking to get away from their kids for a few overpriced nights. Once he cut the ribbon a few feet in front of him, he'd be the first lizard to open a donut shop in Scalestown. He had settled on the name

Donuts on Blanch. The logic was simple—he was selling donuts on Blanch Street. Several of his friends (acquaintances was probably a more accurate term) cautioned him against the idea. Donuts were not very popular amongst lizards— they were too difficult to wrap their hands around. Mr. Ruggles had a plan to change the size of the donuts as well as a foolproof marketing strategy to make sure he got the message out. While he appeared confident on the outside, internally he had his doubts. Given the lizard he owed money to for the up-front loans on all his businesses, failure wasn't an option.

There was a sizable turnout for the ribbon cutting ceremony. Mr. Ruggles scanned the crowd and saw plenty of familiar faces, including some of Scalestown's most successful business owners. If things with his donut shop went according to plan, he'd be wealthier than all of them. Somewhere in the distance he heard his name. He snapped out of his daydream and scolded himself for not being at a high level of alert at such a monumental occasion. It was Beverly Lowery, head columnist at the *Lizard Daily*—Scaletown's primary source of local news. Mr. Ruggles rolled his eyes—what a jerk this Beverly is, he thought to himself.

"Mr. Ruggles, some consider you a savvy businessman, but opening a business centered around donuts sounds the opposite of savvy. Care to comment?"

Mr. Ruggles flashed one of his signature smiles, a smile that had helped elevate him to the social class he now resided in.

"Well, Beverly, once you've seen what we're doing here, not only will you realize it isn't preposterous, but you'll be rushing to get in line for your fair share of donuts."

Beverly flashed a smile of her own and leaned in close so only he could hear, "I have a message from Daddy Long Tongue. He says your cashier may be a little late today and may not be looking well enough to be in front of the cameras. Next time you make a financial decision without getting his ok, you'll be hearing directly from him." Beverly leaned further back and said louder, so the crowd could hear, "Well, Mr. Ruggles, I guess we'll have to wait and see."

Mr. Ruggles smiled again, but on the inside was trying to compose himself. Daddy Long Tongue wouldn't really seek physical retribution against his cashier, would he? After all, Mr. Ruggles had gotten his permission for the donut shop. Sure, there may have been one or two things he left out, but nothing that warranted violence. Mr. Ruggles cut the ribbon to a round of applause. He walked inside to give the tour and show off a couple of different donut flavors they'd be offering. The crowd seemed pleased about the bite-sized donut holes that allowed them to wrap their little hands around them. He saw a member of the press snap a picture of a young lizard with a solid stream of jelly dripping down his chin looking delighted. Mr. Ruggles glanced over to find Beverly so he could give her a smug look, but she had ducked out of the shop. Mr. Ruggles counted down the minutes until he could close the shop, all the while thinking of Daddy Long Tongue.

Overall, it was a very successful day. The grand opening was well received, and in one day he tripled his projected earnings for the entire week. He knew he had to be proactive with the Daddy Long Tongue situation. On his way out the door, he packaged up a couple of his best-looking donuts and tied a bow around them as a gesture of respect to the lizard that ran all of Scalestown, regardless of who knew it. He took a deep breath knowing full well that his night was about to get very unpleasant.

Chapter 2

The cashier woke feeling sore and confused. Where was he? And why? As he looked around the room, he realized his tail was tied to a chair to prevent him from moving too far in either direction. He appeared to be in a dimly lit kitchen. He could hear the dull hum of an old refrigerator and the mixed smells of various spices that ought not go together. The cashier, Jason Alfonso, reached up to feel the back of his head. He was in a considerable amount of pain. Given how short his arms were, he could only feel part of it. He didn't need to feel the entire surface to notice the swelling as well as the feeling of warm blood trickling down his snout. Just then, an oversized, rather unintelligent looking lizard walked into the kitchen. Jason decided to lie still until he got a better feel for the situation. The oversized lizard reached into the fridge and pulled out the supplies to make a savory sandwich that instantly made Jason realize just how hungry he was. When was the last time he had eaten? Next, the oversized lizard reached into what looked like a breadbox and pulled out a bag. He looked and groaned in utter disappointment upon realizing all that was left in the packaging was two end slices. He threw the bread and its corresponding sandwich supplies in the trash with a hint of fury. What a life, to be end slices of bread, Jason couldn't help but think. Your sole purpose is to keep the other pieces of bread from getting stale and when you finally think it's your turn to get eaten, someone throws you in the trash because they'd rather be hungry than consume you. While Jason was by no means a fan of the end slices of bread, he thought the reaction of the oversized lizard was a bit extreme—but that could also have been because of the current state of his empty stomach. After letting out a string of vile words that aren't worth repeating, the oversized lizard began calling to someone in another room.

"Hey Vladdy," the lizard shouted slightly louder than what was necessary given the proximity of the kitchen to the adjacent room.

"Yeah?" Vladdy shouted back, clearly not pleased that he was being disturbed.

"Any word on when Daddy Long Tongue is supposed to get here?"

"Soon, within the hour," replied Vladdy.

Jason shuddered. Daddy Long Tongue coming here? Jason had heard unpleasant stories about Daddy Long Tongue but had never encountered him. Why would he? Jason was an ordinary lizard that lived an ordinary lizarding life free of any vices or activities that Daddy Long Tongue would be interested in. The oversized lizard replied back to Vladdy, "Good, I can't wait for him to meet Ruggles' cashier."

Chapter 3

Daddy Longue Tongue's real name was Dustin Tisburry. No one was foolish enough to call him that, outside of his own mother, of course. He was driving down Doris Avenue going the speed limit. He certainly didn't need to. He could drive whatever speed he wanted, and no law enforcement official would say a thing. He started out in this line of business out of pure desperation to put food on the table and to help pay back his mother's overdue hospital bills. Thinking back to those hospital visits and the sight of the burned scales after his mother's accident still made him feel woozy. What choice did he have but to take matters into his own hands? The job stocking produce at the local supermarket wasn't going to pay those bills and the local Scalestown government certainly wasn't going to pitch in. So, Dustin started hustling to make a buck here and a buck there until he built the realm that all Scalestown now resided in—whether they liked it or not. This situation with Mr. Ruggles was a peculiar one. After all, it was Mr. Ruggles who took him in after his mother's death. It was Mr. Ruggles who taught him work ethic and self-discipline both in business and in life. As Dustin progressed down his career path, Mr. Ruggles neither supported nor lectured him. Dustin was hesitant the first time Mr. Ruggles came to him for a loan. His car wash had fallen through as had his fast-food restaurant. He came to Dustin because his reputation as a successful entrepreneur was starting to diminish. Dustin told Mr. Ruggles it was a bad idea to get mixed up in business dealings together given the nature of the way he operated. Mr. Ruggles was so certain of his future success, he convinced Dustin that it wouldn't be an issue. And it hadn't been. Until now.

Dustin pulled his car into the narrow driveway. He opened the car door, letting the warm air wash over him. As it did, the door to the entrance way of the house opened. Dustin could see the outline of a large lizard and knew it was Pauric. He didn't care much for Pauric, to the point where he hadn't bothered to learn what Pauric's last name was. He was crass and not all that bright but was muscular and followed orders. When dirty work was needed, Pauric was the guy that was often tasked with rolling up his sleeves and getting the job done. Vladdy, on the other hand, Dustin liked very much. Not only were his business and cyber security skills sharp, but his ability to wine and dine Scalestown's elite was invaluable to the operation. When Dustin needed a second opinion, Vladdy is who he turned to. While Dustin didn't know much about Pauric, he knew a great deal about Vladdy. Vladdy had grown up in a large city many miles west of Scalestown. He had dual degrees in Finance as well as Information Technology. After college, he came to Scalestown and took an entry level job at a bank approving loans for lizards looking to stretch their financial means by making purchases they did not need. Vladdy quickly moved up the ladder. At one point, he discovered a technical glitch in the bank's network that could jeopardize a lot of customer data if exposed. When he alerted IT, they laughed him off and told him to go back to approving loans. One night, in frustration, Vladdy was ranting to a friend at a local Scalestown bar about the incident while sipping on a gin and tonic (Dustin was more of a scotch lizard himself). An associate of Dustin's happened to overhear the conversation and put the pieces together that there could be some serious money to be made. The lizard came to Dustin with the information and foolishly tried to play hardball demanding up-front payment in exchange for providing the tip. Dustin sent Pauric to meet with this lizard to help change his mind that an up-front payment was necessary. The associate, rather unenthusiastically now that all he was getting out of the deal was not having to put up with Pauric again, set up a meeting for Dustin and Vladdy. They met at a nice restaurant in downtown Scalestown. There was an immediate connection as Dustin admired Vladdy's quick wit and charisma. Vladdy knew when to draw the line between getting a laugh and showing the proper respect someone like Daddy Long Tongue warranted. After a few drinks, Dustin and Vladdy worked out a plan for Vladdy to hack the bank's system and hold customer information for ransom. According to Vladdy, the bank would be so inclined to recover the data and keep the incident quiet from the likes of Beverly Lowery over at the *Lizard Daily* that they would pay a hefty price. The heist went as planned and Dustin gave Vladdy a fat stack of cash as well as a full-time job offer to become part of his enterprise. It didn't take much convincing—one job and Vladdy experienced a thrill and payout that sitting behind a desk could never provide.

Pauric walked down the front steps to see if Dustin needed help with anything. Dustin waved him off and pretended to be fishing for something in the center console. He needed a couple of minutes to think about how to handle this delicate situation and the last thing he needed was Pauric breathing down his neck.

Dustin closed the center console and swung the door shut. Pauric asked him how he was doing or made some inconsequential observation about the weather; Dustin was not sure, nor did he care. No one knew about his history with Mr. Ruggles. He debated telling Vladdy so that he could get a second opinion on how to handle the situation but decided against it. Dustin never let his guard down to show vulnerability and had no plans on starting any time soon. Pauric reached the front door first and turned the handle, opening the door widely so Dustin could squeeze by. The house was even hotter than it was outside. Pauric called out, "Hey Vladdy, boss is here."

Vladdy hurried into the kitchen and said his hellos. He had gotten new glasses that Dustin had been meaning to compliment. He had given up the half-moon spectacles commonly seen in the banking industry and replaced them with thin rectangular black frames. It made him look younger and hipper, without sacrificing his intellectual vibe. Compliments could wait. Vladdy pointed to the corner of the room where a rather scrawny lizard was laying with his tail tied to a chair. This must be Mr. Ruggles' cashier.

"Pauric," Dustin said, "please wake our friend. Vladdy, step into the other room—I'll be right in."

Both men nodded and prepared to carry out their assignments. Pauric walked to the kitchen to fill up a large bowl of water. As the faucet was running, Dustin closed the door behind Vladdy. It wasn't that Dustin didn't trust Pauric, but the fewer people knew about what was going on in Dustin's mind, the more of an advantage he had over the other movers and shakers in Scalestown.

"My guy called. Mr. Ruggles is on the way," Vladdy said. "Do you think he pulled this little stunt on purpose?"

Dustin sighed, "My guess is he saw an opportunity to make a few extra dollars that no one would notice or care about without realizing the larger implications. Afterall, we told him to use Haverfords as his donut supplier, but we didn't tell him why."

"He still should have done as he was told," Vladdy retorted.

"Yes," said Dustin. "Yes, he should have."

"So, what's the game plan?"

It was something Dustin had been working on in his mind the whole way over.

"Mr. Ruggles is a good lizard—"

Vladdy interrupted, "A good lizard that disobeyed your orders and could end up costing us thousands."

9

Dustin shot Vladdy a look that shut him up.

"He's a good lizard," Dustin continued. "We'll send a message with the cashier, have him get rid of his other supplier and make amends with Haverfords. We'll also tack on an extra tax on all his businesses. If the Haverfords relationship can't be fixed, we'll hike that tax way up."

Vladdy didn't look convinced but knew better than to question his boss. He nodded and asked if that would be all. When Dustin nodded back, he opened the door back up.

Pauric had splashed several bowls of water over the cashier's face. He was now looking attentive and confused with his head cocked slightly to the side, like a dog hearing its name being called but not recognizing the voice.

"Do you know who I am?" Dustin asked.

The young cashier nodded, trying to conceal his fear, without much success.

"You've met my associate Pauric. He is going to strike you in the jaw now."

Before the sentence could sink in, Pauric had landed a blow across the lizard's jaw. Dustin could feel Pauric's excitement pulsating throughout the room. The young cashier let out a howl of pain.

"Sorry about that. Do you know why you're here? Dustin asked, already knowing the answer.

The cashier shook his head, looking as confused as ever.

Dustin asked, "What's your name?"

The cashier paused, glancing around the room, hesitant to give up the information. Pauric landed a blow to the cashier's stomach. Dustin exchanged a look with Vladdy, signaling to make a mental note to remind Pauric later that he did not act until being told to do so.

"The man asked you a question," Pauric said menacingly.

The cashier looked up and said as quickly as he could, "Jason Alfonso."

As barbaric as Pauric could be, you couldn't argue with the results. And in Dustin's line of work, such results are key to success. Just like successful corporations, Dustin was managing a brand. The brand was, of course, himself and it consisted not only of fear but also an understanding from the Scalestown community that he had their best intentions at heart, which was often true.

"You work at Mr. Ruggles' new donut shop, correct?"

Jason Alfonso nodded again.

Dustin continued, "Mr. Ruggles made a few bad business decisions. That is why you're here, Jason. He's on his way over and if we reach an agreement, you'll be on your way shortly. I apologize that you need to be involved but hope you understand. Pauric, one more before Mr. Ruggles gets here for good measure."

Dustin turned towards the kitchen and heard another loud crack and a dull whimper. Pauric was good at what he did, there was no denying that.

Chapter 4

Mr. Ruggles extended his scaly finger towards the doorbell and pushed much harder than was necessary. The sound the bell emitted was unexpectedly weak. It was not the type of sound Mr. Ruggles expected. When he pressed the doorbell, he assumed he would hear the gates of hell itself opening, something so sinister that all the lizards in Scalestown would drop to their knees and attempt to cover their ears to avoid hearing it. For a split second, it alleviated some of his fear. That feeling quickly dissipated upon seeing the large brutish figure that opened the door. Mr. Ruggles immediately recognized Daddy Long Tongue's hired muscle—Pauric. Though limited, every interaction he had with Pauric up to this point had been relatively pleasant. The stories he heard suggested otherwise. The look on Pauric's face did not indicate this would be a pleasant occasion.

Pauric was silent as he opened the door. He extended his arm and made a mocking gesture of politely ushering Mr. Ruggles into the house. Directly in front of him stood Daddy Long Tongue's number two in command, Vladdy. There was something about Vladdy that Mr. Ruggles didn't like. At first, he thought it was because of Vladdy's arrogance but upon further reflection, he realized it was jealousy. Mr. Ruggles liked being the smartest lizard in the room and often that wasn't possible when Vladdy was present. He was sharp, there was no denying that.

Mr. Ruggles saw something moving out of the corner of his eye. Jason Alfonco, his young cashier and first employee at Donuts on Blanch, was tied to a chair, writhing in pain. Mr. Ruggles could see how swollen his face was, even from the kitchen. Pauric's doing, no doubt. Anger outweighed fear and reason, as Mr. Ruggles turned and rounded on Vladdy.

"What's the meaning of this!" shouted Mr. Ruggles at Vladdy. "This is how you treat a valuable business partner?"

Pauric started moving towards Mr. Ruggles.

"Don't come near me you giant ugly piece of—." The door to the other room opened before Mr. Ruggles could finish insulting Pauric. The giant's face was livid with anger as he balled up his hand into a fist.

Dustin emerged, "Thank you for swinging by on such short notice, Mr. Ruggles. No serious damage has been done to your employee, and, assuming you can calm down to have a rational conversation, no further harm will come to him. Please join me in my office. Vladdy, two scotches."

Mr. Ruggles took a second look at Jason before heading into the office. A glass of scotch didn't sound half bad.

"Dustin, what the hell is going on here? You beat up on an innocent young lizard, why?"

Outside of his mother, when she was still alive, Mr. Ruggles was the only lizard that could get away with calling Dustin by his legal name.

"You went behind my back and disobeyed my instructions. I specifically told you to use Haverfords, Inc. as your supplier for everything at Donuts on Blanch. I couldn't have been clearer," Dustin said.

"The company I signed with, Glaze Haze, will save me a significant amount of money each week. It was a smart decision," Mr. Ruggles replied.

Dustin countered, "Were you planning on factoring in those savings when you paid me my fee? Or were you planning on pocketing the extra money yourself?"

Mr. Ruggles fell silent. There was no point in trying to deny it.

"I told you to use them because they offered to bring me in on a much larger operation that could make me more money than your donut shop. Some things are bigger than you, and I shouldn't need to explain my decisions. Haverfords is threatening to pull out of our other agreements because they're worried that I don't have as much power in Scalestown as they originally thought."

"Ok," Mr. Ruggles said. "This could be a simple, civil conversation. Why'd you have to get Jason involved?"

"Because, a representative from Haverfords is on his way to the house now. An example needed to be made and it was either your face or his. Whose would you have preferred?"

Another awkward silence as Mr. Ruggles did not answer.

Dustin continued, "When the representative gets here you will apologize for the misunderstanding and call up your contact at Glaze Haze and cancel while he's in the room. On the call, you're going to explain that you have to cancel because of a prior arrangement with me."

Mr. Ruggles started thinking about his conversation with his supplier. He had made it seem like he was in charge of the operation.

Vladdy knocked on the door and entered with their drinks. He waited for a head nod from Dustin as his cue to leave the room. He got one quickly.

"How's everything outside of business, Mr. Ruggles?" Dustin asked.

Mr. Ruggles was hardly in the mood for small talk, but what choice did he have?

"There's not much else for me outside of business. I'm sure you can relate."

Dustin nodded. He could relate. "How about any lady lizards in your life? Or male?"

"No, I'm afraid business has gotten in the way of pleasure in that sense." Mr. Ruggles replied.

Mr. Ruggles had been in love once before. It was with Dustin's mother, Darlene. It was shortly after Dustin's father, Tobias, had walked out on the family. He had an affinity for gambling and wasn't very good at it. It seemed as though he genuinely loved his family, but he couldn't stop placing bets. It was almost as if he had to do it. If there was a word for this type of behavior in the lizardin, it certainly wasn't well known. Mr. Ruggles had gone to high school with Darlene, so he had known her for many years before the degenerate that was Tobias entered her life. Though they were acquaintances in high school, they were never overly close. Darlene tended bar at the Fly Swatter—one of a handful of bars in Scalestown's limited night-life scene. Mr. Ruggles would take business meetings at a booth in the back-right corner underneath a portrait of a lizard using its tongue to swat a fly clear out of the night sky. They got to talking and eventually started spending more time together. Darlene was insistent that they keep their feelings, and actions, a secret. She didn't want the Scalestown rumor mill churning stories about how quickly she moved on from Tobias. Some may even go out on a limb and assume it was an affair that started years ago and was the reason Tobias packed up and left town.

The other reason she didn't want it to be known was because of Dustin. He was young and was having trouble with the fact that his father wasn't coming home, let alone trying to comprehend a new lizard spending time with his mother. Mr. Ruggles was so infatuated with Darlene that he had little choice but to keep it a secret like she wanted. He was supposed to see her the night of the fire but instead went to a business networking event downtown. Mr. Ruggles convinced himself that he took Dustin under his wing because of the love he shared with his mother, but guilt factored in as well. Would things have been different had he been there that night? Dustin, of course, knew none of this, and Mr. Ruggles had no plans to ever tell him.

Vladdy knocked to inform them that the Haverfords representative had arrived.

The representative from Haverfords was short and plump with a wrinkled forehead and sharp eyes. He looked composed, aside from the sweat drenching through both his undershirt and button-down. He waddled into the kitchen and extended his hand for Dustin to shake.

"Welcome to Scalestown, Mr. Trulio. We appreciate your visit very much," Dustin said.

"I'm Douglas Trulio," the Haverfords representative said, caught off guard that Dustin knew who he was. Vladdy must have done his homework.

"Welcome," Dustin repeated. "This is Mr. Ruggles. He started Donuts on Blanch and would like to apologize for his clerical error in cutting Haverfords out of the supply chain and cancel his deal with his other supplier. Over there you'll see his cashier, Jason Alfonso. We brought young Jason here to make it evident that there are consequences for those who go against orders."

Douglas Trulio, with a great deal of effort, turned around to take a look at Jason. He nodded to indicate that he was content with the punishment that had been doled out. He showed no emotion—this was not Haverfords first time dealing with shady business practices.

"Mr. Ruggles was it? I didn't catch your first name."

"No one does," Mr. Ruggles replied.

Trulio looked taken aback. He glanced around the room, and when he didn't see a reaction from Dustin or Vladdy, he shrugged his shoulders and continued on.

"Consider your clerical error forgiven. Make the call to cancel with your other supplier right now and we'll pretend none of this happened."

Mr. Ruggles pulled out his cell phone from his front left pocket. Given that he was trying to maintain his reputation as an elite businessman in Scalestown, he really should upgrade to a newer version. He pulled up the phone number for Karim, his contact at Glaze Haze, and placed the call. He held the receiver close to his ear, hoping he could somehow convey his message differently if the people in the room could not hear the other end of the conversation. Right on cue Dustin requested he put it on speaker phone.

"Hello?" Karim's voice was friendly and unassuming with a hint of an accent Mr. Ruggles couldn't quite place.

"Good evening Karim, it's Mr. Ruggles calling."

"Mr. Ruggles! Great to hear from you my friend. I hear you blew out your opening day projections!"

"Yes," Mr. Ruggles replied, "We had quite the eventful first day. Unfortunately, there's more to my call than just celebrations. I regret to inform you that I'm canceling our contract and bringing on a new vendor to replace you."

There was a pause on the other end. Mr. Ruggles always found it best to deliver bad news quickly and directly.

Karim's voice hardened. "What the hell are you talking about? You have a month supply already on site that we sent to you for free, and we agreed to a 24-month contract at a more than reasonable price."

"There was a mix-up and another contract was already in place with a different provider," Mr. Ruggles said.

17

Karim replied, "I thought you were in charge? How does something like that happen?

"It was Daddy Long Tongue who had made the arrangements."

"Daddy Long Tongue?" Karim sounded incredulous now, "He can wrap that long tongue around my nuts. You told me that bozo worked for you, Ruggles."

Mr. Ruggles turned bright red. A serious line had been crossed. He kept his eyes on the phone to avoid making contact with anyone. He heard a dull thud and a muffled cry of pain and looked up. Pauric had his hand around Jason's mouth and had just delivered a well calculated blow to his groin. Mr. Ruggles allowed his eyes to meet Jason's and then hover over to Dustin's. For the first time, Mr. Ruggles did not feel like that paternal figure who had stepped in to help mold an intelligent young mind— instead he felt like countless others that Dustin had delivered that look to: terrified and helpless.

"Mr. Ruggles," he reminded Karim. No matter how ugly the situation, Mr. Ruggles was determined to cling to that one piece of dignity—being addressed formally. "I'm afraid I misinformed you. I, along with the rest of Scalestown, work under Daddy Long Tongue's domain."

"My friend," Karim began, "I'm surprised to hear you let him push you around."

Dustin had kept his silence long enough. "Mr. Ruggles does not *let* me do anything. I do what I want, when I want. This is Daddy Long Tongue. I'll give you thirty seconds to apologize for your crude comment about where I could wrap my tongue or else my associates and I will be heading in your direction to force an apology."

There was a short silence on the other end. Technically, Karim did not operate in Daddy Long Tongue's territory. He must have weighed it over and determined it was not worth having this beef because he replied, "My friend. I have nothing but respect for you and your operation. I do indeed apologize for my comment. It was directed in frustration towards Ruggles. Mr. Ruggles that is. I'd love to have a tongue like that, yeah? I'd be making friends with lady lizards three blocks away."

"This conversation, like your contract, is over. Best of luck in your future endeavors, Karim," Dustin said before slapping Mr. Ruggles' phone off the table, which did an effective job of both instilling fear in the audience as well as ending the call.

"Pauric, give the cashier a ride home. It's too hot of an evening to have him walking. Vladdy and Douglas, please wait for me outside."

When it was just Mr. Ruggles remaining, Dustin turned and rounded on him. "If it wasn't for the guidance you gave me growing up, you'd be dead right now. There will be no more warnings. Moving forward, what you've done in the past doesn't matter. I'll bury you myself."

Mr. Ruggles nodded in agreement, "Completely reasonable. I screwed up."

Dustin continued, "You'll start receiving shipments from Haverfords in three weeks to get your operation back up and running."

"Why not let me use the one month supply I already have from Glaze Haze? It was free."

"No, you're shut down and you'll eat the costs," Dustin replied.

"Dustin, I know you're upset, and rightfully so, but let's not let emotions get in the way of good business. Closing up shop for three weeks hurts both of our pockets."

Dustin knew that Mr. Ruggles was right. His reasons for shutting down the operation were petty in the grand scheme of things.

"Fine, use up the free month's supply to keep the shop up and running. But your tax goes up to for the month while you use Glaze Haze."

"Fair enough," Mr. Ruggles replied.

As soon as Mr. Ruggles exited the house, he reached for his cell phone to call back Karim. The call was picked up on the first ring.

"Karim, it's Mr. Ruggles. I'm alone now."

"Oh yeah? And why should I believe you?" Karim replied.

Mr. Ruggles rolled his eyes, "Daddy Long Tongue can wrap that long tongue around your nuts."

Karim burst out laughing. A genuine deep laugh that Mr. Ruggles could feel through the other end of the phone. "You embarrassed me. I have to take crap from that bozo because of you? He's lucky I'm not driving up to Scalestown right now to teach him some manners."

Mr. Ruggles refrained from telling Karim that it would not be a good idea to come to Scalestown. Karim talked tough, but Mr. Ruggles had a hard time picturing him winning any sort of physical altercation against Pauric.

"Listen," Mr. Ruggles started, "I convinced Daddy Long Tongue to let us finish up using the one-month free supply you provided me. I know he was emotional, but, when it comes to business, he can be very rational. Haverfords needs three to four weeks to ramp up production. That gives us time to get Scalestown enjoying better tasting donuts before being forced to consume whatever low-quality garbage Haverfords will come up with."

"I guess we'll have to wait and see, my friend."

Chapter 5

Jason was still in a state of shock driving down back roads with Pauric at the wheel. Pauric insisted that Jason sit up front next to him. Jason would have done just fine in the back, away from Pauric's stench and singing voice. It was hard to believe that this thug of a lizard knew the lyrics to some of the hottest pop hits currently topping the charts. Jason was trying to figure out which was the worst—the stench, singing, or driving.

Maybe it was the singing that was the worst. Jason tried to block out the painful tune in order to focus on his next challenge. How was he going to explain his highly visible injuries to his girlfriend, Cassidy? She had been pushing him to take classes at the local community college, but Jason was easily distracted by the sight of a quick buck and chose to work for Mr. Ruggles instead. He wondered if he'd get the look of concern or the told-you-so look that she often, unsuccessfully, tried to mask when she knew she was right. Most likely a combination of each. No matter what he said she'd be suspicious and concerned about why he was out so late and why he was so bruised up. He decided he'd just have to tell her the truth. As Pauric pulled in the driveway, Jason realized his phone had died. He had no idea how long ago. Knowing Cassidy, there could be a special operations team out looking for him right now given how long he'd gone without contacting her. Jason reached for the door handle and the locks clicked, preventing him from getting out.

"What, I don't even get a kiss goodnight?" Pauric said with a dumb grin on his face.

When Jason didn't reply, Pauric unlocked the door and said, "Get the hell out of my car you little shit." Jason did not need telling twice.

Jason made his way for the front door. He was already dreading this conversation with Cassidy. In fact, part of him wished he was still in the car with Pauric. The door swung open with the force of a Category 5 hurricane. Cassidy's face was a mix of concern, rage and then confusion. Jason could feel her eyes focusing in on the swelling on his face and the blood that was still trickling down his head.

"Jason! Where have you been? What happened to you?" she burst out crying and flung herself into his arms.

Jason winced in pain. "I'm ok, let's get inside and I'll tell you all about it."

Jason filled Cassidy in on all the details. As he started speaking about it, he was glad he had her to talk to. It sounded so bizarre as he explained it out loud, even though he had just experienced it. Cassidy sat still with her jaw slightly dropped, patiently waiting for Q&A. When Jason recounted the last detail he could recall, she began digging in her purse and pulled out her phone.

"What are you doing?" Jason asked.

"Jason, we have to call the police right away. They're criminals and should be locked up," she replied.

"Absolutely not Cassidy. Put your phone away right now. We'd both be in danger. It's out of the question."

Cassidy paused while she thought it over and then seemed to conclude that he was right.

"You'll quit in the morning then," she stated.

"No, I won't," he replied, "I'll go to work in the morning and act like it never happened. It's the only option."

He walked past her to head to the kitchen to get some ice for his throbbing head as she muttered a comment under her breath about how this wouldn't have happened if he went to college. He chose to ignore her. His head hurt too much already; bickering may cause it to explode.

But Jason didn't head to work the next day. He got an early morning call from Mr. Ruggles checking in on him. Mr. Ruggles apologized profusely and told him to keep track of any medical expenses to be reimbursed. He also told Jason to avoid coming back to work until his face healed, but that he would still get paid. It was slightly touching to have Mr. Ruggles offer that up, but Jason knew he was trying to avoid customers seeing his battered face.

"Are you sure? Who will run the register?" Jason asked when Mr. Ruggles was done speaking. "Mathieu cannot cook the donuts and run the register at the same time."

"Don't worry about that. I can run the register or hire someone to fill in part time. We'll make sure Mathieu is only focused on baking."

Chapter 6

Mr. Ruggles hung up the phone. He was frustrated. It had been such a good opening day. Oh well, what's done is done and now it's on to day two.

He was heading to the shop even earlier today. He had paid two teenage lizards to swing by to get a couple of free boxes of donuts to bring to their schools. Getting in with the high school crowd was important to the success of the shop. Donuts on Blanch didn't close until 11pm—significantly later than any other establishment in Scalestown that did not serve alcohol. Mr. Ruggles' plan was to have high school students not only stop in before their first classes of the morning but also later in the evening while out and about on the town searching for mischief. During those hours, he planned on creating a hip vibe with live music and a fun atmosphere. Without much to do in Scalestown, he was hoping this could fill the void. High school students weren't necessarily flush with cash though. Their parents, however, oftentimes were. Mr. Ruggles knew it would be important to build credibility at the parental level as well. He was planning on hitting PTO meetings, church volunteer groups, and youth sporting events on the weekends to spread the word. The final audience that Mr. Ruggles wanted to crack into was the retired community of Scalestown. Bored and looking for some sort of fulfillment to pass the hours until death came knocking at their doors, this group could be quite profitable as well. He planned on stopping by the nursing home in Scalestown as well as waiting outside the Scalestown Diner to hand out samples to older lizards. The Scalestown Diner wouldn't like this customer poaching, but Mr. Ruggles didn't care. The thought of taking customers away from a competing business invigorated him. High school students in the early morning, older lizards around 8-9am, parents picking their kids up from school or shepherding them around to different activities, and then the same high school crowd looking for some form of entertainment. Mr. Ruggles' plan accounted for attracting business at every portion of the day, as well as every day of the week. It was time to make some serious money as well as cement his legacy as one of the greatest business figures Scalestown had ever seen.

Chapter 7

All things considered, Scalestown was a pretty modest place. Most of the town was residential, consisting of small homes with front lawns for young lizards to play on. While it wasn't an overly wealthy town, it hadn't fallen into the same hard times as some of the surrounding lizarding communities. A lack of jobs and increase in crime had taken its toll on nearby areas. At one point it looked like Scalestown may be heading in that same direction. The project to revitalize the downtown area coupled with a decrease in crime were key to avoiding that fate. Mr. Ruggles played an important role in a project to revitalize the downtown area by revamping it to attract lizards to spend their paychecks in Scalestown instead of other places. He helped lobby the mayor at the time, Gene Louis, to cut taxes for local businesses. Soon afterwards, Mr. Ruggles started his first company, tax free.

The downtown was shaped like a baseball diamond. Two main roads ran through the middle of it—Doris Avenue and Blanch Street. At the center was a park with a playground for children, benches for adults, and oftentimes food carts for lizards of any age who needed a mid-day snack. If the park was the pitcher's mound, the police station was home plate. Down the first base path was the fire station, library, and city hall. If you crossed Doris Ave and continued down the right field line, you'd pass a gym called 'Buffs'. Working out had become a recent craze in Scalestown and other surrounding communities. A well-known doctor and professor, Dr. Arthur Verner, had published a study showing a direct correlation between getting regular exercise and living a happier, healthier life. Directly next to Buffs, at the tail end of Blanch Street, was Mr. Ruggles donut shop—Donuts on Blanch. Crossing Blanch Street would bring you to the equivalent of the outfield on a baseball diamond. There were two bars and a bowling alley. The first bar, Wild Wilma's, attracted a younger crowd. If someone of Mr. Ruggles' age was in there after 9pm, they'd stick out like a sore thumb. Next to Wild Wilma's was The Wharf—a more upscale bar serving cocktails instead of cheap beers. Next to The Wharf was a bowling alley that needed a new coat of paint and updated decor. Mr. Ruggles was highly considering this as his next investment after Donuts on Blanch was up and running. After the bowling alley you'd cross Doris Ave and get to the dry cleaners that Mr. Ruggles also owned. If you continued down the left field line, you'd pass the diner before getting to the other end of Blanch Street. Once you crossed Blanch Street, you'd be on the third base path headed towards home plate. On that stretch, you'd find a jewelry store, barber shop, and bank.

There was more to Scalestown than just the downtown of course. If you continued southeast on Doris Avenue, you'd get to a grocery store, department store, and a movie theater. Just south of that was a neighborhood where a lot of Scalestown's younger residents lived, including Jason Alfonso. It was affordable yet close enough to downtown that you could stumble home if you had a few too many drinks. If you left downtown in the opposite direction and headed northwest on Doris Ave, you'd get to the Scalestown schools. Because it was a small town, elementary through high schoolers were all in the same two buildings next door to each other. When Mr. Ruggles was growing up, sports in Scalestown were a big deal. The fields would be packed, and the competition would be fierce. Over the past few years, however, it seemed like the intensity and participation levels had dropped off. Why that was, Mr. Ruggles did not know.

If you headed southwest on Blanch street out of downtown, you'd get to Mr. Ruggles' construction company. The area was heavily wooded and, unless you lived there, lizards didn't have much of a reason to head out in that direction. Mr. Ruggles lived on the outskirts of downtown in between the schools and his construction company. If you headed northeast on Blanch Street leaving downtown, you'd pass a doctor's office and a dentist's office. If you continued up the road you'd get to a rather large stream. Lizards of all ages would gather here when the weather was nice to enjoy the water. Further up that road, you'd eventually get to Daddy Long Tongue's residence. Most people never saw it, but it was one of the nicest homes in Scalestown.

The other contributing factor to Scalestown avoiding a downward spiral was the dip in its crime rate which Daddy Longue Tong was largely responsible for. As he rose to power, robberies and vandalism decreased and there were fewer rival criminals attempting to jockey for position. One could question how accurate the current crime rate was, however, given that Daddy Long Tongue had influence over the police department, press, and city hall.

Chapter 8

The door opened and two high school students walked into Donuts on Blanch. Mr. Ruggles was in the kitchen speaking with Mathieu when he heard the bell signaling someone had entered the store. He instructed Mathieu to finish the batch and bring it out front when it was ready. Mr. Ruggles walked out of the kitchen and greeted the two teens with a smile and a handshake.

"How are we today, boys?" Mr. Ruggles asked. He always found it awkward trying to connect with teenage lizards. Does he shake their hands? Give them a high five? A first bump? Avoid any physical contact all together? They were at such a different stage in life and sometimes it was difficult for him to remember what he was like at that age.

"We're good, thanks," the shorter of the two lizards replied. "Are the donuts ready?"

"My chef will be bringing them out any second. Have you tried one yet?"

"No, not yet," replied the short lizard. The tall lizard was awkward and gangly and did not seem capable of speech.

"Well, here then," Mr. Ruggles said, "try these while we wait."

The two teenage lizards bit into the donuts, and both of their faces lit up.

"Holy shit these are good," the gangly lizard exclaimed. He blushed and apologized for his foul language.

Mr. Ruggles chuckled, "No need to apologize, I'm glad you like them. Remember, hand them out to as many of your classmates as you can. Do that, and you both can have free donuts for a month. How's that sound?"

The two young lizards looked at each other and shrugged. It seems like they were going to ask for cash up front but, after tasting the donuts, were fine with payment-by-snack instead. Mathieu walked out of the kitchen with four boxes.

"Here you go," Mr. Ruggles said. "Feel free to take some of these stickers and put them up around the school as well."

The boys picked up the boxes of donuts and crammed a couple of stickers hastily in their pockets on the way out the door. The shop would open in fifteen minutes. The gangly boy had not shut the door properly, so Mr. Ruggles walked over to close it. As he started to do so, he glanced out the window and saw a line forming all the way down Blanch Street.

Mr. Ruggles squirmed with excitement. "Mathieu, head back to the kitchen, we're going to have a busy morning."

Like the first day, the second was a blur. Mr. Ruggles was planning on heading down to the nursing home at some point but, with Jason out, he never had the chance. He hardly had the chance to use the restroom and his lunch consisted of a bag of peanuts washed down by some room-temperature iced tea. Mathieu's day must have been equally as hectic, Mr. Ruggles thought. Part of the plan was to have the donuts made fresh every morning, but if the first two mornings were any indication, that may not be possible. They may have to make some the night before to be able to meet demand.

Mr. Ruggles thanked Mathieu for his hard work and told him to head home and get some rest. Mathieu insisted on staying to help, so the two went to work cleaning up the entire kitchen in silence. Once the kitchen was cleaned, Mr. Ruggles walked back up front to the register and started counting the money.

Mathieu's jaw dropped in disbelief as Mr. Ruggles pulled out the bundle of cash from the register. It was significantly more than day one. Mr. Ruggles thought about giving Beverly Lowery over at the newspaper a call but decided against it.

Chapter 9

Jason was born and raised in Scalestown, not too far from where he currently lived with Cassidy. His childhood was pretty typical. Both of his parents worked, so they were never short on money, but they were by no means wealthy either. His mother was a librarian with a passion for educating the Scalestown youth about classic literature and poetry. Jason was never a fan of either. His mother would make him read book after book and, when each one concluded, they would sit down to discuss the characters and the underlining themes and lessons that were woven into the pages. Jason's father was a locksmith. Jason would accompany him to work some Saturday mornings if his mom was teaching a class at the library. He'd sit in a chair against the wall behind his father's desk and listen to Scalestown residents come in and explain how they had lost their keys.

Jason was an only child but lived in a neighborhood with plenty of lizards his age. Some of them he was still friends with today. There was never a lack of activities, games or adventures to embark on. Jason's parents were never big into sports, but Jason enjoyed them quite immensely. At his games, other parents might complain about the officiating or the ridiculous play calling from the coaching staff while Jason's parents would sit calmly and nod along politely. His mother, in particular, challenged him academically. She wanted him to excel in the classroom to arm himself with a wealth of knowledge. What he did with that knowledge, however, was up to him. She never pushed him in a certain direction when it came to his future.

When Jason was seventeen, his parents decided they wanted to retire and move south to enjoy warmer weather. They were originally going to wait until Jason graduated high school and went off to college, but his father got a great offer to sell his locksmith business and they were able to sell their house for more than they would have dreamed. His parents invited him to join but were not surprised when he declined. He had a steady girlfriend, Cassidy, and was heading into his senior year of high school. Instead of moving south with his parents, he moved in with his aunt and uncle on the other side of town. They had never been particularly close. Most nights, Jason would sneak up the back-stair way at Cassidy's to spend the night. He'd have to get up just before the sun rose to make sure he could vacate the premises before her father got up to head to the office.

Jason was qualified to go to college, but after his senior year he opted not to. If there was one thing his mother had instilled in him, it was that every lizard must choose his or her own path and such decisions should not be made rashly. After graduation, he and Cassidy moved in together. She went to college while Jason found odd jobs to help pay the rent all the while claiming he would go back to school soon. Much to her chagrin, he still had not and was now working at Donuts on Blanch.

Early the next morning, Jason's phone rang. He heard Mr. Ruggles voice on the other end.

"Jason?" he asked, almost sounding panicked. "How's your face looking?"

Jason replied, "It's starting to feel better. It's still not looking very public-facing though."

"That's fine, Jason. I need help in the kitchens today. You'll be out of view of any customers. Can you make it?"

"What about Mathieu?" Jason asked.

"Yesterday we were so busy he couldn't even clean any dishes. Can you make it in today or not?"

Jason hurried upstairs and turned on the shower. Cassidy walked out of their bedroom still half asleep. "What's going on?" she asked Jason.

"Mr. Ruggles needs me to come into work today. I won't be in front of people, I'll be cleaning dishes out back."

Concerned, Cassidy asked, "Do you feel up to it?"

"I don't think I really have a choice, Cass."

Jason tapped softly on the back door and was greeted by Mathieu who smiled and let him into the kitchen. Jason had been surprised to see a line already forming outside the shop; he assumed he'd be able to walk right in the front door. Mathieu glanced at Jason's face and looked concerned. Jason mumbled that he had tripped and bumped his head on a park bench and that he was fine.

Mathieu seemed like a good guy, but he didn't know him that well. What he did know was that Mathieu never tried anything he made. He was such a perfectionist that he'd discover a flaw no matter what.

"Was it this busy yesterday?" Jason asked.

"Yes," Mathieu replied with a smile.

Jason's eyes flickered down to the batch of donuts Mathieu had just finished making. He hadn't eaten breakfast and his stomach was starting to growl. He should have eaten something at home. Mathieu noticed and picked one of them up and offered it to Jason.

"Please, give this a try," he said, again with a smile.

Jason accepted. He took a bite in and was caught off guard. It was the first of Mathieu's donuts he had tried. Jason couldn't believe how delicious it was. He ate the rest of it in another bite. Now he understood the lines that were wrapped around the corner.

"What you think?" Mathieu asked.

Jason grinned back, "These are amazing! No wonder it was so busy yesterday."

The door to the kitchen opened and Mr. Ruggles walked in. His eyes took stock of Jason's face. There were signs of both guilt and disappointment. Perhaps he looked guilty because his disappointment wasn't genuinely about Jason's health, but instead about the health of the operation if Jason wasn't able to get behind the counter.

"Gentlemen! Ready for another exciting day? The line outside is even longer than yesterday so we have our work cut out for us." Mr. Ruggles' energy was palpable. Jason and Mathieu nodded to indicate they were up to the challenge.

"Great!" Mr. Ruggles continued, "Today is all about efficiency. There are both repeat customers as well as new customers in line. We need to provide the same level or service and wait time as we did our first two days. Jason, I'll stack dirty dishes on this windowsill here. Try to keep your face out of sight—you need to be more careful my young lad! As the dishes come through get them cleaned and laid out for assembly of the next batch. Any questions? Ok! I'm off to open the door!"

Mr. Ruggles hurried out of the kitchen and marched over confidently to the front door and turned the sign around to indicate Donuts on Blanch was open for business. The day went by quickly enough. There was a never-ending flow of dirty dishes that needed cleaning. As soon as Jason finished a batch, another five or six plates and utensils would come back through the windowsill. Jason and Mathieu barely had time to interact. They each got a 15-minute break in the afternoon to eat some lunch. Mathieu had packed some fresh vegetables with hummus. Jason, of course, had forgotten to pack a lunch and didn't have time to run out to a deli, so had to settle for another donut. It wasn't the worst thing to have to settle for he supposed. By the end of the day, Jason and Mathieu were drained. Even Mr. Ruggles' normal energetic, confident demeanor was dialed back a bit. This was only a weeknight, too, Jason thought. What would happen on the weekends when they were open later? Jason realized that at this pace, Mr. Ruggles would have to hire more help.

When Jason got home, he greeted Cassidy at the door with a quick kiss and a hand squeeze but that apparently wasn't enough. As they sat down to dinner, Cassidy made it clear that something was on her mind. Jason sighed to himself. He was getting too old to play games. After awkwardly dancing around what was upsetting her for a solid ten minutes, it finally bubbled up to the surface. She was upset that he agreed to go to work that morning. She was upset that he decided to go back to work at Donuts on Blanch after the incident. She was upset that he took the job in the first place instead of going back to school. Jason nodded along but the whole time was counting down the minutes before he could lie down and pretend to sleep. Tomorrow, he'd be back in bright and early to resume duties in the kitchen. As they got into bed, Cassidy mentioned they should start going back to Temple. Jason rolled his eyes, which, of course, only upset Cassidy more. Now she was upset that he wasn't taking it seriously; that they needed guidance and strength given Jason's run-in with Pauric and Daddy Long Tongue. To appease her so he could get some sleep, he agreed to go to Temple that weekend, all the while knowing there was a very good chance that Mr. Ruggles would need him to work multiple shifts.

Chapter 10

Mr. Ruggles sat back in his chair. Another long day. His feet were sore, as was his back. His pride was also a bit wounded. There were some lizards who talked down to him thinking he was a mere cashier. Mr. Ruggles wanted to jump over the register and exclaim that he was the owner, a visionary, and a much bigger success then they'd ever be. He wanted to ask what they did for work. How much money did they have in their bank accounts? He started to get worked up all over again and had to remind himself that it didn't matter. After a third straight day of staggering results, Mr. Ruggles had brought in more cash than he expected to for the first two months. He was in the process of listing out and prioritizing what he should use that excess cash on. His top priority, he knew, was to hire more head count. He needed a permanent dishwasher, another cashier and probably another chef. Maybe he'd pay the boys a small bonus to show how much their hard work was appreciated. Build some loyalty and trust early on. Not a bad idea, but he didn't want to get carried away. While the first three days had yielded results far beyond his expectations, Mr. Ruggles needed to stay conservative with his spending. Over-spending early on in business ventures had hurt him in the past. What to do about Glaze Haze though? The only thing that compared to the importance of money was his reputation and being forced to back out of the Glaze Haze deal would damage it. As he was thinking it over, the phone rang.

"Hello?" Mr. Ruggles answered.

"My friend! How are you?" Mr. Ruggles recognized Karim's voice on the other end of the line.

"Hello Karim, I am well, thank you."

"How's business my friend? Are you selling donuts?" Karim asked.

"Almost faster than we can bake them," Mr. Ruggles replied.

"Good, good that's great. It must be the Glaze Haze, yeah? Too bad you're going to cut us off."

Mr. Ruggles rolled his eyes. "It is a shame, Karim. I think after a few more successful days I should be able to go to Daddy Long Tongue and present a case that it's worth staying with you guys."

"Ok, buddy. Get some rest."

Mr. Ruggles thanked him and said goodnight. Tomorrow, Mr. Ruggles would have to put a help wanted ad out in the *Lizard Daily*. He should probably ask Jason and Mathieu if they had any friends looking for work as well. Always better to have a candidate who has a stamp of approval from an existing employee. He also wanted to know how much longer Jason's face would look the way it did. Mr. Ruggles wanted to continue his marketing efforts by reaching out to some of the other targeted groups to get them interested but hadn't had a chance to leave the donut shop, thanks to the impact Pauric and his meaty claws had on young Jason's face. He reached his hand out for a last swig of his scotch and knocked the glass off the side of his desk. The scotch spilled onto the dark grey rug. Mr. Ruggles jumped up and ran to the kitchen to get a sponge and some cleaner. He had purchased the rug off a foreign lizard who was passing through Scalestown that had claimed it was one of only a few original Claude Matisse designed rugs left. The lizard had asked if Mr. Ruggles was familiar with Claude Matisse. Mr. Ruggles had acted insulted—what a silly question to ask a lizard of his stature. The seller had apologized and said that since Mr. Ruggles knew and respected Matisse, he could sell it at a discount. The truth was Mr. Ruggles had never heard of Claude Matisse but knew the name would be good to reference at a dinner party. Over the years, Mr. Ruggles had showed it off many times and not one person had heard of Matisse either. Even though he knew he had most likely been duped, Mr. Ruggles was still very fond of the rug. By the time he had scrubbed Claude Matisse's masterpiece clean, it was close to 2am. Mr. Ruggles' body was ready for bed, but his mind was still quite active. The last time he remembered seeing on the clock was around 2:45am. Another grinding day lay ahead.

Chapter 11

Jason woke up before his alarm went off at 6am. He got up and crawled quietly out of bed, jumped in the shower, put his clothes on and was ready to walk out the door when Cassidy walked out into the kitchen. She was typically a pretty heave sleeper.

"You weren't going to say bye?" she asked, visibly angry.

"I didn't want to wake you," Jason said, although he had trouble convincing himself it was true.

She looked at him skeptically, "You're going to ask Mr. Ruggles about getting Sunday off for Temple, right?"

Jason sighed, "We'll see Cass. I've only worked there for a couple of days and we're crazy busy. I feel awkward asking for a day off already. But if the opportunity presents itself, I'll ask."

"Fine," she said. "Are you going to eat breakfast?"

"No time! I'll just grab a donut at the shop. See you later, love you!" Jason replied as he rushed towards the door.

Jason had no intention of asking Mr. Ruggles about Temple. His face was nearly healed though. It had healed up surprisingly quickly. The swelling had decreased and the colors of burst blood vessels in his forehead were starting to blend into his naturally dark colored scales. Jason anticipated looking like a beaten sack of potatoes for another week at the minimum. Still, he doubted he was in good enough condition to be behind the register. Another day of furiously scrubbing dishes he supposed. But it was a paycheck—and got him out of the house.

Chapter 12

Dustin lifted his leg up, so his foot was resting on the top stair of his porch to make tying his dark brown dress shoes easier. His mother used to poke fun at him because he still tied his shoes using the bunny ears method as opposed to the loop-swoop-and-pull technique. That's the way she had taught him, and he hadn't seen any reason to change his tactics over the years. He stood up straight, put on a silver wristwatch, adjusted his tie, and ran a hand through his hair to make sure it wasn't sticking up. He had a big meeting with Douglas Trulio and his superiors at Haverfords' headquarters to finalize their most significant business deal. Dustin never liked getting dressed up. That was something more for Mr. Ruggles or Vladdy. The amount of money riding on this meeting made it a necessity.

Haverfords was a massive company. Dustin wasn't even sure everything they did. It ranged from automobile manufacturing to food processing to household cleaning supplies to home surveillance equipment and beyond. Rumor had it they were even working on the prototype for a flying car. The company had identified a problem in the communities surrounding Scalestown. Each town, aside from Scalestown, had a water treatment facility to ensure the water its residents drank was safe. These facilities were expensive to build, operate and maintain. Scalestown did not need one because the quality of the water that ran through the town's large stream was pure enough to consume as is. Haverfords wanted to build out the infrastructure to supply nearby towns with Scalestown's water. Haverfords would charge these towns a high price, but that price would be cheaper than the cost of running their own treatment facilities. Haverfords would pay Scalestown large sums in taxes to operate and access the water. On paper, it made sense for all parties.

Douglas and his team had tried going through Scalestown's Better Business Bureau to get approval. The Scalestown officials passed on the offer because it would involve shutting down the stream from the public, which they were not prepared to do. Douglas had gotten word of Dustin's influence in Scalestown and reached out to see if anything could be done. Dustin told Douglas that he could get the Bureau to approve the project. Douglas' superiors were skeptical and asked Douglas to do a trial run with Dustin to see how he operated. That's where Donuts on Blanch came into play. Dustin shook his head thinking about how Mr. Ruggles' greed almost blew up the whole deal. He'd now have to convince the top executives at Haverfords that something like that wouldn't happen again and that they'd have access to the water supply as requested. The truth was Dustin hadn't brought the issue to his contacts at the Bureau just yet. Before asking for that type of favor, which would undoubtably cause pushback from the Scalestown community, he wanted to have an official deal with a dollar amount.

Dustin walked down the porch towards Pauric's car. Pauric was waiting diligently next to the passenger side door, ready to open it for him. Vladdy sat in the back seat. As he got closer, Pauric opened it, allowed Dustin to get in, and closed it with surprising tenderness as if tucking a new-born lizard into its crib.

A song came on the radio. Pauric chuckled out loud. When no one asked him what was so funny, he chuckled again—a little louder this time.

"You ever been thrown out of a concert, boss?" Pauric asked Dustin.

"No, Pauric. I don't believe I have," Dustin replied.

When it became evident no one was going to ask him why he asked the question, Pauric continued, "I got thrown out of a concert once. Well, hell, a couple of times now that I think about it. But one of them was seeing this band." He motioned to the radio, "This song was playing at the exact time. You believe that?"

Vladdy finally relented after a long pause, "Well, are you going to tell us what happened or not?"

"So, I'm there with a friend. Well, not really a friend. I knew the guy. I think he gave me the tickets because he was scared of me. Or maybe I told him to give me one. I don't remember. Anyways, I go up to the bar to get a couple of beers, and I turn around and see these three lizards giving him a hard time. They wanted to stand where we had been standing. It was a prime spot. Front and center. Great view of the band and of a couple of girl's asses dancing right in front of us. The guy I was with, he was trying to stand his ground but wasn't much of a fighter. So, then I walk over. You know me—I'm not going to put up with that. So, I walk over, and I ask them what's up? They're three pretty big lizards. Not as big as me. But big. And there were three of them."

Dustin wondered how long this story would drag on for.

"So, I look at them and ask them if they think they're tough. Now they see the rage in my eyes, and they start looking a little shook. One of them said something to me. I don't remember what it was, but he said something. So, I chug my beer staring at him the whole time. Then I raise the one I bought for my friend and I chug that one too. Then, I headbutted the guy square in the face. He dropped flat to the ground. I turn and headbutt his buddy in the face too. The third lizard makes a run for it to get security. Two security guards walk over and ask me to leave. I say yeah ok, after this song. Two pricks look at each other. Then they look at the two lizards lying on the ground bleeding everywhere. They look at me and

44

shrug and say ok, one more song. So, the song finishes. I pat my buddy on the back and they escort me out."

Pauric finished his story as they pulled into the Haverfords parking lot. At least it passed the time.

The Haverfords headquarters were quite modest. While it looked like a normal company on the outside, Dustin knew from Vladdy's research that it was far from it. They were as crooked as he was, just operating under an LLC with streams of legitimate revenue trickling down to the bottom line to provide some level of cover for their illicit activities. Pauric opened the door for Dustin and Vladdy. They had talked about whether to leave Pauric in the car. No doubt, Douglas had told his superiors about the beat down Pauric had put on the cashier, Jason Alfonso, so they figured they'd let the Haverfords team put a face to the name. While they permitted Pauric to join them, Dustin had made it very clear that he wasn't supposed to speak. No matter the situation, Dustin had said, a handshake and a head nod should suffice.

They walked down a narrow hallway to an opening to a larger room that required you to walk down three short steps. Dustin wondered how much effort it took Douglas Trulio to get up and down them. The waiting area had portraits of several important looking lizards on the wall—none of whom Dustin knew anything about. The walls were beige, and the furniture fit in nicely with the theme. There were two love-seat sofas as well as a less comfortable looking plastic folding chair. On the far end of the waiting area was a receptionist who had failed to notice their entry. His hair was grey and thinning on top and he, like Douglas Trulio, was overweight. Dustin, Vladdy and Pauric walked across the room. The receptionist still did not look up. The three men stood in an awkward silence in front of the desk. It appeared as though the older man had fallen asleep in his chair. If it weren't for his heavy breathing, one could have mistaken him for being dead.

Pauric stomped his foot and the man sat up with a surprising quickness. Perhaps this wasn't the first time he had been caught nodding off on the job.

"Gentlemen! I apologize, I was buried so deeply in my work I didn't even hear you come in. What can I do for you?"

Dustin had to hold back from laughing and could feel Vladdy doing the same. "We have a 2 o'clock appointment with Douglas Trulio, Manuel Jacques and Richard Tarley."

Looking puzzled, the receptionist stated that he did not think any of them were in the office at the moment but that he'd double check. He reached towards the phone on the desk, picked up the handle, and started dialing a 4-digit extension. He lowered the phone slightly.

"And what's your name, sir?"

"Dustin Tisburry."

He hung up the phone and tried another extension. After a similar amount of time he hung up and dialed a third number. As the phone was ringing, a look of stress was visible across his face. Again, no answer.

"None of them answered. Feel free to sit and wait," he said, using his hands to gesture over to the group of chairs.

"Perhaps you could try them again," Vladdy interrupted. "We have a very busy day."

"Of course," the man said, "I'll try again right now." He went through the same process without any luck. He shook his head and raised his hands to shrug to imply he was just as confused as they were about the Haverfords executive team's absence.

Dustin lead the trio over to the couches.

"Who the hell do these guys think they are?" asked Pauric, fuming.

"He's got a point," Vladdy interjected. "This is a partnership and it's time they started acting as though we're equals."

Before Dustin could respond, the telephone at the receptionist's desk rang. He reached for it automatically and answered on the second ring. He remained on the line for just over a minute before hanging up.

"Mr. Tisburry," he called out while motioning him over to the desk. "That was Mr. Trulio, he said they'd be arriving in fifteen minutes and apologized for the delay."

Dustin nodded and headed back over to his seat to relay the news to Vladdy and Pauric. There was no small talk. They waited in silence.

Fifteen minutes later the door opened, and Douglas Trulio waddled through the entrance. In his wake were Manuel Jacques and Richard Tarley. Manuel was thin with a beige turtleneck sweater tucked into dark slacks. Richard looked fit. He had a traditional suit on and looked like he belonged in the upper echelon of business executives. While Richard was indeed fit, Pauric still dwarfed him— something Dustin was pleased about.

"Apologies for the wait," Douglas said to Dustin and Vladdy. He took a quick look at Pauric before diverting his eyes. Images of the damage to Jason Alfonso's face were no doubt still lingering in his mind. "This is Manuel Jacques and Richard Tarley."

Dustin extended his hand and shook Manuel's hand and then Richard's.

"Gentlemen," Dustin began. "Thanks for meeting with us and for approaching us with this business opportunity. We're very excited about working together. I'd like to make one thing clear," Dustin continued with an air of politeness, "while you're powerful lizards in a powerful company, this is my town and I don't wait for anyone. Don't be late to another meeting with me again. Now that we've established that, let's get started."

47

Manuel and Richard exchanged surprised looks; they were not used to being addressed this way. They looked at Douglas, who gave them a nod indicating this is what they should expect working with Daddy Long Tongue.

Chapter 13

When Jason walked into Donuts on Blanch, Mr. Ruggles was there talking to Mathieu. Mathieu looked uncomfortable and was not saying much. Mr. Ruggles either didn't notice or was just charming enough to carry the conversation on his own.

"Jason, my boy! How are you feeling?" Mr. Ruggles asked.

"Morning, sir. I'm feeling great. Hi Mathieu," Jason replied.

Mr. Ruggles continued, "Your face looks great! It's healed up nicely. Maybe a little bit of a scar. We'll see. I'm sure the ladies will be fighting over you and your ferocious new look. Oh, wait you have a nice little girlfriend don't you. What's her name again?"

"Cassidy."

"Cassidy that's right, that's right. Lovely young lizard she is. Well I do say I think your face looks well enough to get behind the register today. What do you say Jason? Are you up for it?"

"Absolutely, sir. That's great news," Jason responded.

"Ok, great. I need to make the rounds today to help spread the good word around the community about our donuts. We have another dishwasher starting this morning to help lighten the load. I'm interviewing candidates to help Mathieu in the kitchen, as well as a back-up cashier and potentially a delivery boy or girl depending on how these meetings today go. What an opportunity we have, boys!"

Mr. Ruggles has charisma, Jason thought to himself. It was easy to see how he has been so successful in his business career.

"Where will you be going today, sir?" Jason asked Mr. Ruggles.

"I'll be heading to the Nursing Home this morning and then Buff's gym after that. This evening I'll be going to a PTA meeting at the high school to see if we can get donuts on the menu."

Jason was jealous. These donuts were a hell of a lot better than the grub he got back when he was at Scalestown High.

"Alright boys, I'm off. I'll check back in late afternoon and then be back for the evening. Mathieu keep it up. Jason, you're in charge while I'm gone. Remember, we're making a name for ourselves so put the customer first. If anything urgent comes up, call my cell phone."

Jason had not expected to be left in charge. It was a little intimidating but also a good opportunity to prove himself to Mr. Ruggles.

"Oh, and one last thing, Jason," Mr. Ruggles called back over his shoulder. "Can you attend Temple on Sunday and bring three boxes of donuts? I'd like to be able to sell them our donuts for their Coffee Hour after the service. Much better than the cheese and crackers they lay out now. Although I guess I haven't been to Temple in some time so who knows. Thanks Jason, now I'm off for good."

Before Jason could respond, Mr. Ruggles was out the door. Jason chuckled to himself – guess he will be going to Temple after all.

Chapter 14

Mr. Ruggles walked into the nursing home. While the lizards that were housed there didn't have much disposable income, their friends and family that came for visits would surely rather munch on one of his donuts instead of the food that was served. The menu at the nursing home may be worse than Scalestown High's. The nursing home wasn't as depressing as Mr. Ruggles had envisioned. There was a bingo game going on to his left and a group of lizards watching a television program to his right with the volume turned up to a piercing level. There was another group playing cards and yet another deep in conversation, looking over their shoulders discussing the latest gossip from around the home. Mr. Ruggles walked over to the group playing bingo with two boxes of donuts under his arms.

"The wisest of all Scalestown residents!" he exclaimed to the group. "My name is Mr. Ruggles. I opened up a new donut shop in town and figured I'd give out some as a thank you for all you've done for the community over the years."

A couple of the elderly lizards nodded in approval while a couple looked around at each other confused and unsure who this well-dressed lizard was and why he was interrupting their game. He handed out a donut to each of them and watched as they began to bite in. A woman in her late thirties walked up behind him and tapped him on the shoulder.

"Can I help you?" she asked.

"Well hello! I was giving out some treats out of gratitude to these esteemed lizards of the Scalestown community. My name is Mr. Ruggles, I own the new store, Donuts on Blanch."

The woman's eyes lit up. "Oh my. I had one the other day and couldn't believe how tasty they were. It's great to meet you. Due to dietary restrictions, not all of these lizards should be eating sweets."

"Margaret!" she suddenly shouted. "You know you're not supposed to eat sweets."

Margaret pretended not to hear and took another bite into the donut.

"I apologize," Mr. Ruggles said. "I should leave this to the experts. Can I leave this box with you and you can hand out to those allowed to consume them? Also, is there someone here from management I could speak with?"

"What, a young female lizard can't be in management?" she asked while folding her arms.

"Oh my of course not, of course not. It's just not common you meet someone in management who has such direct contact and knowledge with patients. Very impressive, very impressive indeed."

She smiled back, "I'm not a manager. But I can grab Donna."

Mr. Ruggles smiled back, "That would be great, thank you. Make sure you take one or two of these for yourself," he said with a wink.

"I'll be sure to. It was a pleasure meeting you, Mr. Ruggles," she said as she walked through a door behind the desk to go and fetch her boss.

A few minutes later, Donna came through the door and out around the desk. Mr. Ruggles recognized her immediately but couldn't place her. Based on her expression, he could tell she knew who he was. At least her name had been mentioned so he could act like he remembered.

"Mr. Ruggles, it's great to see you again," she said with a firm handshake.

"Donna! How lovely to see you again, as well," Mr. Ruggles played along. "When was the last time?"

"It was the Better Business Bureau holiday party last year."

Now Mr. Ruggles remembered. She had been recognized for an award for holding a management position at the local hospital—the first female lizard to do so.

"Of course, how silly of me. You've moved on from the hospital then?"

"Yes," she replied. "I'm now Executive Director here and report straight to the CEO."

"That's wonderful. What an accomplishment!"

"Thank you, Mr. Ruggles. I hear your new donut shop is off to a very hot start? I'll admit I have yet to make my way over there," Donna said.

"Yes, we're doing quite well out of the gates. Some people scoffed at the idea, but I'm sure you've dealt with doubters and scoffers your entire career."

She beamed, "I certainly have."

"Here," Mr. Ruggles said opening the second box of donuts he had brought. "Give one a try."

"Why thank you," she said as she extended her hand into the box and pulled out a chocolate glazed. She bit into it and her eyes lit up the same way they did when she was discussing her career accomplishments.

"Oh my. These are divine!"

"I'm glad you think so," Mr. Ruggles replied. "I was actually hoping to partner with you. I think our donuts could bring some joy to your residents and some comfort to those visiting loved ones who may have seen better days."

"It's an interesting idea. I'm not sure if we have the budget for it," Donna replied.

"Do you have an office we could step into Donna? I'm sure we could hash out some sort of agreement," Mr. Ruggles said with a warm smile.

Chapter 15

The line of people waiting for their orders was growing. Jason poked his head into the kitchen. Mathieu was working ferociously to keep up with demand. They were at peak hours for the before-school crowd. The store was packed with teenagers representing the different social circles that made up Scalestown High. A few lizards in baseball shirts who were waiting on their orders started to get restless. One had picked up a metal napkin dispenser and started tossing it to one of his friends. The friend caught it and then threw it back even faster. This time, it was bobbled, and the napkins fell out and scattered over the floor. A third friend chimed in with some profane insults mocking the lizard who had dropped the dispenser.

Mathieu had just placed three more donuts out on the windowsill for distribution. Jason called out the numbers over the microphone.

"Are you kidding me? Where the hell is our order?" one of the lizards in baseball gear moaned to his friend.

Jason took a deep breath. Mr. Ruggles had said put the customer first. He was close to snapping on these spoiled little brats.

The three friends started throwing the napkin dispenser back and forth again.

"Hey guys—knock it off, will you?" Jason called over.

"Blow me!" shouted back the ringleader.

Jason leapt over the counter with surprising agility. The kid took a half step backwards, not expecting it.

"You're going to leave now. And you're not allowed back," Jason said in a menacing voice. He was enraged and doing everything he could from backhanding this little punk.

The kid looked around at his two buddies, unsure of what to say. He was trying to play it cool, but Jason could tell he was scared.

"I played for Coach Pierce a few years ago when I was at Scalestown High. I don't think he'd be too pleased to hear about your behavior, do you? I've seen lizards kicked off the team for much less," Jason said.

Mathieu hit the bell to indicate an order was ready. Its ring broke the awkward tension. Jason turned and read off the number. It was this lizard's order. Without breaking eye contact, Jason picked up the donut and ate it in front of him.

"Have a great day, boys," Jason said sarcastically as the three baseball players hung their heads and turned and walked away. As they left, the other two friends began chastising the instigator for getting them kicked out.

The rest of the morning went smoothly enough. After the high school kids left, the retirees came in with their newspapers and crossword puzzles. They cleared out around 9:30am. Jason and Mathieu finally had a chance to take a deep breath and use the bathroom. It would remain somewhat slow until lunch when working lizards would come in for a treat before heading back to their cubicles for the rest of the day. Around 3:00pm, parents would stop in with their kids on the way home from school. After dinner, it would be more families coming for dessert. After 7, it would be lizards in their twenties and thirties socializing. Some with coworkers, some with friends, and some on first dates. Could they find love sweeter than the chocolate glazed donuts? Time would tell.

While the diversity of customers kept things interesting, each group made Jason feel like a failure in their respective ways. The high school kids showed him no respect. The elderly crowd looked as though they were holding back from telling him to stop wasting his time and do something productive with his life. The parents looked at him with hesitation wondering if this same fate could await one of their children. The lizards his own age seemed to not even notice he was there. He was a different breed; a different species put on the planet to perform a basic transaction to provide them with a brief moment of pleasure. Jason couldn't decide which was the worst.

Chapter 16

"Twelve and a half percent!" Vladdy exclaimed as Pauric whooped in agreement.

"Keep your voice down, Vladdy. We're still in the parking lot," Dustin replied.

"Sorry boss—but twelve and a half percent? Come on! We were saying we would have settled for five percent."

Dustin lowered his voice in the hopes Vladdy would match his volume, "Yes, I think we made out very well for ourselves."

The negotiations had gone quite smoothly and were over quicker than Dustin had anticipated. Haverfords would pay to have a dam built to separate the stream into two sections so that young lizards did not lose their entire area to play when the sun was out and so Scalestown did not lose out on revenue of families visiting the area. They'd use a labor force made up of Scalestown workers to build the dam. Politicians were always looking to be able to say they helped create blue collar jobs. Dustin could already picture the headlines and quotes that would take over the front page of the *Lizard Daily*. This would build up good will with the community and the local government and put more money back into the town's economy. The next stop for Dustin would be to pay his friends at City Hall a visit to get them on board with the plan. Over the years, he had built solid relationships with government officials that helped enable his success. He didn't think it should be an overly difficult task. Dustin had worked with them on trickier situations than this and was always able to get things done.

Chapter 17

The nursing home was almost too easy. Mr. Ruggles used his charm to convince Donna that his donuts were just what the nursing home needed to keep visitors happy. Afterall, Mr. Ruggles argued, it was typically visitors that paid the bills. Throughout the conversation, he continued to stroke Donna's ego about all the wonderful accomplishments she had achieved throughout her career. He also invited her to join a networking dinner with some of Scalestown's most prestigious business lizards which delighted her. Now, it was time to stop by Buff's and then the PTA meeting and then head back to check on Jason and Mathieu.

Mr. Ruggles pushed open the door to Buff's Gym. He was met with a smell of sweat and damp towels. There were several very fit young lizards in cut-off t-shirts with heavy weights in each hand. They each had headphones in and were immersed in their exercise routines. Their bodies appeared to be treated as temples, and Mr. Ruggles doubted they would be enjoying donuts after a workout. Further in the distance, Mr. Ruggles could see some heftier lizards who were trying to get into better shape. Their doctor had no doubt told them about Dr. Arthur Verner's study on how good exercise is for lizards and how it could increase life expectancy by a certain percentage Mr. Ruggles could not recall. These were the folks that would take a donut on the way out of the gym. They wanted to listen to their doctor and family, but they'd be too tempted to pass up on the savory sweets. They'd convince themselves they had taken good enough care of their bodies that day and deserved a reward. Surely, Dr. Verner would agree if he were present. As he was taking in the scene, Mr. Ruggles saw Gary Dupler walking down the staircase from the second floor. Gary was the owner of Buff's and was the man who Mr. Ruggles came to meet. Gary and Mr. Ruggles had gotten into it a few times at town hall meetings around how best to spur economic growth in Scalestown. While the conversations could occasionally get a little testy, there was a level of mutual respect that each had found ways to be successful entrepreneurs in a town that did not have a strong history of producing them. Gary had always been a health nut and his body reflected that. He was probably only a few years younger than Mr. Ruggles, but a stranger passing by on the street would never guess it. Where Mr. Ruggles had some excess fat hanging over his belt buckle, Gary had visible abs when his tight shirt was tucked neatly into his pants. When Dr. Arthur Verner released his study on the health benefits of exercise, Gary latched on. He appeared on the news and was interviewed in the local papers discussing the benefits of exercise. Soon after, he opened the first gym in Scalestown. Another thing Mr. Ruggles and Gary had in common was who leant them money for their first business ventures—Daddy Long Tongue. Buff's was on Pauric's weekly collection rounds.

Gary extended his hand and shook Mr. Ruggles' vigorously. His hand was quite sweaty. Mr. Ruggles made a mental note to wash his hands in the restroom before he left.

"Mr. Ruggles, great to see you. How're things?" Gary asked.

"Gary, great to see you as well. The place looks great. Things are good on my end, busy but good. Thanks for taking the time to meet with me."

"Of course. You mentioned on the phone you had some business to discuss. I have to teach an aerobics class in 15 minutes—let's hear what you got," Gary replied.

Mr. Ruggles wasn't sure what an aerobics class was but, never one wanting to look uninformed, did not inquire further. "I'd like to partner up. I bring donuts from my new store over for your customers to grab and enjoy on their way out the door."

Gary scoffed, "Absolutely not. The whole point of the gym is to help lizards live healthier lives. Bringing in sweet treats like your donuts would be the opposite of the brand we've been building."

"Gary, think it through. Right now, the majority of lizards in here look like warriors. How many warriors do you see walking around Scalestown? To really expand, you're going to need to attract average lizards as part of your clientele. You can't expect the every-day-Scalestown resident to completely change their lifestyles and dedicate their lives as if they were preparing for war. Your message should be to work hard, love yourself, and reward your efforts by enjoying life's finer treats."

Gary's eyebrows raised in an amused fashion. He appeared to be thinking it through. "Always the salesman, Mr. Ruggles. So, what are you proposing?"

Mr. Ruggles replied, "We drop off a fresh batch of donuts every morning and you get 30% of the daily profits."

Gary countered, "We try it out at three days a week and we split 50-50."

Mr. Ruggles scratched his chin and gave the illusion he was thinking over the offer. He really just wanted to get his product exposure to this group of lizards. He did not need it to be a large revenue stream in the long run. A 50/50 split still worked out in his favor. After another thirty seconds of appearing to mull it over, Mr. Ruggles replied, "Done." The two lizards shook hands and Mr. Ruggles headed towards the exit as Gary Dupler walked in the opposite direction to his aerobics class—whatever that meant.

Chapter 18

It was around 5:30pm and Jason was exhausted. Mr. Ruggles had said he'd be back after the PTA meeting around 6:00 to relieve Jason of his duties. Given the steady flow of traffic, he wasn't sure if Mr. Ruggles would be able to send him home or not. Thankfully, a second dishwasher and cashier were starting tomorrow. Jason would get to have top pick of hours and the new cashier could take what was left. Poor Mathieu though—Mr. Ruggles had not found a back-up chef and, Jason thought to himself, may not be looking for one given Mathieu's talents. Mathieu did not seem to mind the long hours doing what he loved, however. Jason realized he had, yet again, forgotten to bring a lunch or dinner. He'd need to start remembering to do that. Time to slip back to the kitchen to see which donut looked best for an afternoon snack. He had handed out quite a few Scalestown Banana Cream donuts as well as Doris Ave Delights. He glanced down at a menu to remember which each option was.

Scalestown Banana Cream ~ Raised brioche donut, filled with earl-grey infused banana cream, doused in milk chocolate ganache and rolled in real chocolate jimmies ~

Doris Ave Delights ~ Rich chocolate cake donut with vanilla bean glaze, nutella, and fresh blackberries ~

Both sounded pretty damn good. Jason ducked back into the kitchen and asked Mathieu for one of the Doris Ave Delights. He gobbled it down letting out a sigh of content. "Mathieu, these may be your best yet!" Mathieu looked back sheepishly, grinned and nodded his head in appreciation of the compliment for his craft.

"Have you always enjoyed cooking?" Jason asked Mathieu.

Mathieu nodded, "I had a toy set as a child. Mathieu's Diner. That's what my parents wrote on the front of it. There was a little kid sized booth you could sit at, fake strips of bacon and hamburgers to put in a plastic frying pan, and even fake menus with daily specials."

Jason laughed, picturing the scene.

Mathieu asked, "What about you—do you like to cook?"

"Nope. Not at all. My girlfriend enjoys it, so she cooks a good amount. If not, I'd be getting take-out or cooking frozen pizzas most nights. I liked baseball growing up, but that's a tough one to turn into a career."

"Were you good?" Mathieu asked.

"I wasn't bad," Jason said. "But let's put it this way, no one would be lining up around the corner and paying money to watch me play."

Mathieu grinned again.

Chapter 19

Mr. Ruggles entered the high school cafeteria right as the meeting was about to kick off. The white board at the front of the room had his name as the third agenda item. Before getting to his piece, Mr. Ruggles would have to sit through a conversation on outdated football equipment, as well as a discussion around school bus route efficiency through Scalestown. Ideally, he could go first and miss out on those other two hot topics, but this should be a pretty easy win, so it was worth the time.

A no-nonsense woman got up and welcomed the crowd. She gave a very quick overview of the meeting agenda and set the tone that people should get to their points clearly and quickly. She called up a rather frail looking lizard to kick-off the meeting. Slim and trembling, she did not fit the typical mold of the parent up there looking for new football equipment. She was a nurse and had a very strong talk-track around the increased chances of serious injury when equipment is older than eight years. She cited third party medical publications as well as tugged at the heartstrings by telling a story of her son's friend who could no longer play the game he loved because of an injury sustained while wearing outdated equipment. Cheers broke out across the room as the measure successfully passed. As the woman took her seat, a lizard with short hair and glasses got up to talk about traffic efficiency around the Scalestown school entrances. Mr. Ruggles stopped listening so he could think over what he was going to say. There was some back and forth on the issue of traffic and nothing got solved. The lizard with the short hair and glasses had to take his seat, defeated.

The stern looking woman got up again and this time introduced Mr. Ruggles to the audience. Mr. Ruggles stood, straightened his tie and approached the podium. "Good evening ladies and gentlemen, and thank you for allowing me some time this evening. For those who do not know me, I am Mr. Ruggles. I own several successful businesses in the area and most recently opened Donuts on Blanch, which has been a big hit. I'm here tonight because I would like to partner with the school to offer our donuts through the lunch program at a discounted rate."

The stern woman stood up and interjected herself abruptly into the conversation, stopping Mr. Ruggles in his tracks.

"We've already decided on this matter. We will not be selling your donuts at our schools, Mr. Ruggles. We have longstanding relationships with other suppliers who have our best interest at heart. Thank you for coming in."

Mr. Ruggles stood frozen in an awkward trance in front of the room full of lizards. He felt himself handing the microphone over to the next speaker without putting up much of a fight. The next thing he knew, he was walking down the aisle towards the exit and pushing his way out through the door. He came to his senses by the time he got back to his car. Mr. Ruggles debated leaving and heading back to Donuts on Blanch, but now that he had regained his bearings, he was becoming enraged that he was treated with such disrespect in public. He decided to wait out front of the school for Hal Poland to come outside. Hal was a decent enough guy. Mr. Ruggles knew him from back when he used to go to Temple. He figured he could talk to Hal to see what the hell happened in there.

Twenty-five minutes later, Hal walked out of the school towards the parking lot. Mr. Ruggles emerged out of the shadows and called out to him. Hal look surprised to see him still waiting in the parking lot and looked over his shoulder before walking over.

"Hal, what the hell was that?" Mr. Ruggles asked incredulously.

"I got word it was going to happen five minutes before the meeting started," Hal Poland replied. "I'm not sure who you pissed off, but someone rallied the parents to vote down the measure."

"Can you get them to change their minds?"

Hal Poland started smirking. "Most likely."

"What's it going to cost me?" Mr. Ruggles asked with an audible sigh.

"My kid's birthday is coming up. I want your donut shop to cater it for free. He loves those things," Hal replied without skipping a beat.

"Fine. Send me the details and I'll take care of it. Assuming you can get the parents to change their minds about donuts here at the school."

Chapter 20

Jason was exhausted yet again as he walked up his front steps. It was 11pm and he was just getting home. At least he was going to score some major points with Cassidy around this Temple business. He carefully stacked the donuts on top of the refrigerator and then opened the cabinets to get some food. He was running on a steady diet of donuts and water and it was starting to catch up with him. His eyes scanned through the cabinet trying to identify the necessary supplies to make a peanut butter and jelly sandwich. After grabbing the peanut butter, Jason wrapped his fingers around the loaf of bread and pulled it off the shelf. It felt light. He opened the bag and found just the end slices remaining. His chest tightened as he immediately was back chained to the chair waiting for Daddy Long Tongue to show up. Jason took a couple of deep breaths to try to calm himself down. The panic was quickly replaced with anger—Pauric was right to be mad, the end slices were the worst. He ended up snacking on some cheese and crackers before heading upstairs to brush his teeth and get into bed.

Cassidy stirred awake as Jason pulled the covers back to slide underneath. She mumbled something incoherent without opening her eyes. He kissed her on the forehead and leaned in and told her that he had changed his mind and wanted to do Temple in the morning after all. Her eyes opened, and she let out a cry of triumph. She hugged him and told him multiple times what a great idea it was and how much good it would do him. It would certainly do some good for Donuts on Blanch, that much was sure.

"What made you change your mind?" Cassidy asked the next morning as they cooked a light breakfast. She was wearing a yellow dress and her hair was braided to look more formal.

"I just don't think I fully processed the whole Daddy Long Tongue situation and need a little guidance to get back on the right track," Jason lied.

Cassidy beamed and offered to do the dishes. Clearly, she agreed he had not been on the right track. Jason hadn't been to Temple in years. He never liked going when he was forced to growing up and doubted today would be any different.

The Temple was designed to worship Meelosh and Emil. Thousands of years ago, according to scripture, the planet was inhabited by all sorts of beasts and creatures and Meelosh ruled them all. Over time, a deadly insect breed developed and started killing off life at a rapid rate. With the planet's future in balance, Meelosh created the first lizard, Emil, out of clay to combat the rise of the deadly insects. Emil eradicated the insects, and the planet was saved. According to devout believers, Meelosh chose the lizard to be protector of life—a superior species with vast responsibilities for the livelihood of the planet. Temple was a place to honor Meelosh's power and to celebrate Emil's creation and triumph. Young lizards learn at temple that they must live a pure and wholesome life, like Emil did, in order to be worthy of Meelosh's approval. And, according to scripture, life was not worth living without the approval of Meelosh.

Services usually took about ninety minutes. The first thirty of those minutes are sitting in complete silence. A time dedicated solely for reflection and meditation. The second portion is for the Swatting of the Flies. The preacher rattles off problems with society and the crowd chants, "Strength to Emil" after each one. After the preacher gets through his or her list, members of the Temple could get up and rattle off their problems that they needed help solving. In similar fashion, the crowd, joined now by the preacher, chant back "Strength to Emil."

Those in attendance want to get Emil's attention to focus on the problems that are most near and dear to their hearts. During the final part of the ceremony, the crowd passes around a ceramic sculpture shaped like a fly and every lizard licks it. This symbolizes the hard work Emil did when defeating the deadly insect breed. After everyone has licked the sculpture, the official ceremony ends, and all are invited to stay and celebrate. This is where Mr. Ruggles wanted his donuts.

"Remember, Jason, you've met a decent amount of these lizards before. They know me well since I'm here more often than once every five years," Cassidy said as they got in the car the next morning.

"Who will be there that I've met?" Jason asked.

Cassidy answered, but Jason barely paid attention. He wasn't going to be able to place faces to names anyways. He'd just nod politely to anyone who spoke to him.

"I'm not licking that bowl."

"It's not a bowl, Jason. It's a symbolic sculpture and everyone licks it out of respect and gratitude for what Emil did for this planet," she shot back.

"The fact that everyone licks it is exactly why I won't be. There have to be statistics out there that show a higher rate of disease being spread among temple-goers."

As they pulled into the parking lot, Cassidy said, "You absolutely will lick. Don't embarrass me or, most importantly, disrespect the temple."

Jason shut the car off and got out. He opened the back door and took out two boxes of donuts that Mr. Ruggles had given him as samples. Jason had told Cassidy that Mr. Ruggles was being nice and wanted to contribute to the Temple celebration. They walked across the parking lot and, as they got close to the entrance, she reached out and held his hand. A greeter opened the door and welcomed them to the Temple. It was as bland a building as Jason remembered from his childhood. The seats looked just as uncomfortable as well. Cassidy took Jason's hand and started leading him back to the kitchen to drop off the box of donuts. As they entered the kitchen, a large lizard with an abnormally long tail was washing his hands at the sink.

"Marvin! How wonderful to see you! This is my boyfriend, Jason. Jason, this is Marvin Deholmes. He does a lot of the maintenance and helps run the Temple," Cassidy blurted out.

"Nice to see you again, Marvin," Jason said as enthusiastically as he could muster.

Cassidy shot him a look that implied he had never met Marvin.

"Cassidy, nice to see you. Jason, great to meet you. Are those the donuts from Mr. Ruggles? You can put them on the back table. We'll have an answer for you at the end of the celebration. Now run along and find yourselves good seats!" Marvin said as he hurried off to fix something in the adjacent room.

Cassidy shot Jason another piercing look. What decision? Jason hurried out of the room as he was instructed to while making a concerted effort to avoid Cassidy's gaze.

The service was as painful as Jason had remembered. The first half an hour crawled by. Jason divided his time between pondering how many lizards in the audience actually believed this crap and how he'd be able to get his hands on one of the donuts after the service ended. As they moved into the second portion of the service, Jason would get the occasional sharp elbow from Cassidy when he didn't reply "Strength to Emil" with enough vigor. Then came the ceramic fly. Jason watched as it was handed from lizard to lizard. An elderly lizard coughed violently on his hands before placing them directly on the middle of the fly and giving it a lick. A child placed his tongue on the fly and left it there waiting for his mother to notice that he was drooling on it. After a long forty-five seconds, she glanced down and scolded him, but at that point his drool was steadily dripping down the edges. The child grinned as if he had just broken a personal record. Jason was choking back vomit. Cassidy could be as angry as she wanted—there was no chance Jason was going to come in contact with this disgusting cesspool of Scalestown germs. Finally, the fly made it to Cassidy. She gave a short, quick lick and handed it to Jason. Jason took it from her and handed it to the next lizard without even pretending to lick. The lizard looked back, surprised that it was getting handed to him so quickly. He shrugged and took it from Jason and gave a long lick over the puddle of the kid's saliva. Jason could feel Cassidy radiating with rage and embarrassment. No doubt lizards would talk about this. The young lizard who shows up after years of absence only to disrespect the customs this temple was built upon.

The temple emptied as lizards made their way back to the room where Jason had left the donuts with Marvin Deholmes. Jason did his best over the next twenty minutes to put on a good show for everyone Cassidy introduced him to. When she stepped away to go to the bathroom, he swooped over to the table with the donuts only to discover there were only crumbs left. Bummer.

As Cassidy returned from the bathroom, Marvin Deholmes approached Jason. "Tell Mr. Ruggles he has himself a deal. Forty boxes a week for the agreed upon price. Cassidy, always a pleasure."

Cassidy practically dragged Jason out of there. Once they got into the car she erupted.

"What the hell, Jason!"

"What?" Jason replied, trying to play dumb.

"Everything you said was bullshit. Processing your feelings, becoming a better lizard...it was all bullshit. You came here to conduct a business deal on behalf of that slimy boss of yours."

"You wanted me working harder and making more money. Well, now I'm doing that," Jason replied, although he did feel a pang of guilt. He could have handled this whole situation better. At least Mr. Ruggles would be pleased.

Chapter 21

Hal Poland waved from the back deck. Mr. Ruggles waved back doing his best to feign excitement. There were several ways Mr. Ruggles enjoyed spending his Saturday afternoons—an elementary school birthday party was not one of them. But he had promised Hal he would cater his son's party for free in exchange for Hal convincing the PTA to sell Donuts on Blanch in the school cafeterias. A small price to pay in the grand scheme of things.

Mr. Ruggles opened his trunk to gather the boxes. Hal left out that they were expecting forty lizards at the party. Forty lizards—for a kid's party—really? Jason had packed up Mr. Ruggles' trunk to the brim with boxes. Mr. Ruggles should have brought him along to help unload it all.

The sounds emanating from Hal's backyard were almost unbearable, even from the street. A combination of shrieking, shouting, crying, and laughing mixed in with the dull babble of adult conversation. It was like an orchestra whose conductor had fallen off stage, leaving each section of instruments competing for who could play loudest. Mr. Ruggles walked around the side of the house to deliver the boxes, which were balancing dangerously in his hands. He glanced around the yard and it looked like a warzone. Kids tackling each other, jumping out of swings, running in circles, stray toys abandoned across the lawn like fallen soldiers. Why had he worn his expensive loafers? There was a steady stream of water coming out of an unattended garden hose creating patches of mud. The deck suddenly felt very far away. Mr. Ruggles was going to have to navigate this back yard like it was a damned mine field. If his boxes got knocked over and he had to go back to Donuts on Blanch to get more his Saturday, and likely his loafers, would be ruined.

Mr. Ruggles took a few steps into the warzone. A skinny five or six-year-old jumped in front of him, blocking his path.

"My name is Clooney Scourge and my favorite activity is evil!" the kid shrieked.

"What?" Mr. Ruggles asked, confused.

The kid then kicked him square in the shin and ran off in the other direction laughing like a maniac. A lizard, presumably his mother, called after him, "Lenny! We don't kick! Come back here!"

His shin was stinging, but Mr. Ruggles had managed to maintain control of the boxes. He maneuvered his way through the backyard to get to the deck, all the while on the lookout for Clooney Scourge or Lenny or whatever the hell this lizard's name was that had kicked him. As he climbed the steps to the deck, Hal saw him and came down to help with the boxes.

"Mr. Ruggles! Thanks for stopping by. Great day for a party, isn't it?" Hal asked.

"Hal, next time let me bribe you in cash like a normal lizard, won't you?" Mr. Ruggles replied.

Hal smiled, "Not really your scene, is it?"

Mr. Ruggles smiled back, "No, I can't say that it is."

"Well you're going to be the hit of the party. All these kids love the donuts. Hell, the parents do too," Hal replied.

Hal turned to the party, "Hey everyone! Mr. Ruggles is here with free donuts for everyone!"

The crowd of children erupted in a roar of cheers.

"And how do we thank people who do us nice favors here in Scalestown?" Hal called out, giving Mr. Ruggles a wink.

In unison the crowd of children screamed back, "we sing them the greeny-weiny-grateful lizard song!"

"That's right!" Hal screamed back. "One-two, one-two-three," Hal yelled out while waving his hands.

The orchestra had found their conductor and were performing as one complete unit once again. In perfect unison kids and parents broke into this greeny-weiny song accompanied by a cult-like dance. Neighbors stuck their heads out the windows to join in. Strangers passing by in their cars honked.

What the hell was happening? The song ended and Mr. Ruggles waved to the crowd. He shook Hal's hand and walked off the deck to get back to his car as quickly as possible. He was halfway across the yard, and his loafers were still unscathed thanks to side stepping an empty ketchup packet and leaping over a puddle of mud.

"Lenny! No! Get back here!" the woman's voice rang out.

Mr. Ruggles glanced over his shoulder and saw the kid who kicked him in the shin running after him with a squirt gun. Great. Mr. Ruggles picked up his pace, but the kid was gaining traction. Was it worth the embarrassment of running away from a five-year-old to keep his shirt dry? Based on the size of the squirt gun, Mr. Ruggles decided that it was. He started jogging towards his car. A few steps in, he slipped on some mud and fell over. The kid had caught up with him. His face was triumphant.

He raised his squirt gun to the sky and shouted out, "My name is Clooney Scourge and my favorite activity is—"

"Evil," Mr. Ruggles finished the sentence for him. "Your favorite activity is evil."

The kid looked back at him in surprise. He paused another second before screaming "evil!" and pulled the trigger to his toy gun, soaking Mr. Ruggles and his expensive shirt.

His mother had caught up with them and pulled the gun out of her son's hand. "Lenny! We don't chase old lizards and squirt them with our toys!"

Old? Who's she calling old?

"What do we do when we've been mean to someone Lenny?" the mother asked.

Lenny didn't skip a beat, "We sing the scaley-waley-sorry song!"

Oh no. Not another cult-like song. "Oh no no no. No apologies or songs necessary. I'm sure Lenny here is very sorry."

The kid looked up at his mother. Then at Mr. Ruggles. Then back to his mother. He kicked Mr. Ruggles square in the shin and started laughing before sprinting away, his mother at his heels.

It was worth it though; a few days later Hal ended up delivering and getting the vote changed. Donuts on Blanch would be served at Scalestown schools.

Chapter 22

Dustin woke up early on Monday morning. Vladdy was able to get in touch with two of his contacts at City Hall to arrange a 10am meeting. The plan was to pitch why the dam was good for revenue and the town as a whole. They had thought through all objections and were ready to combat each and every one. At the end of the day it would come down to the money, as it always did. Dustin was very confident that there wouldn't be any issues getting the Haverfords deal pushed through.

They'd be meeting with two men. One was the head of the Better Business Bureau (BBB), Wes Helmstead, and the other was Casper Fitzpatrick, a member of the City Council. Wes was the one who had shot down the Haverfords proposal when Douglas Trulio had presented it. Casper helped Wes get the head job at the BBB. This meant that a proposal of this size surely must have made its way up to Casper. That's why Dustin wanted both of them present. To get the deal through, Wes would have to approve, and it would most likely need a majority vote in the City Council. Truth be told, Mr. Ruggles had better relationships with both men than Dustin did. They exchanged favors and had a mutually beneficial relationship. Dustin's relationship was built on fear. If not for the recent issues with Mr. Ruggles, he probably would have called upon his former mentor to execute this meeting at a country club somewhere while drinking fancy champagne.

Pauric pulled into the City Hall parking lot at 9:45, found an empty spot near the entrance, and parked the car. Vladdy, per Dustin's orders, had made it clear that for this meeting Pauric would be waiting in the car. He got out dutifully nonetheless and walked around the car to open the door for Dustin.

"Thank you Pauric. We shouldn't be very long," Dustin said before he and Vladdy headed down the path towards the front doors. If Pauric was offended at being left behind, he didn't show it.

They entered the building, walked down a straight hallway, took a left and approached a door with "Better Business Bureau" printed across the glass window. Vladdy opened the door and allowed Dustin to walk past him. Unlike the receptionist at Haverfords, this was a younger employee who was much more alert. She welcomed them and, after taking their information, walked them down the hall to a conference room where Wes and Casper were already waiting.

"Gentlemen," Dustin said smiling while extending his hand. "Good to see you and thanks for making time for us."

"Of course, Daddy Long Tongue. Vladdy, great to see you as well," replied Wes.

Casper then extended his hand and embraced both Dustin and Vladdy. "Always happy to meet. We didn't get a ton of details—just that you wanted to discuss the Haverfords water proposal."

"Yes," replied Vladdy. "We're working with them on one or two small ventures and this project came up. Upon discussing further, it sounds like it makes a lot of sense for all parties. Our understanding was that you wouldn't allow the deal to happen?"

"That's correct. It would hurt tourism, revenue and be bad for the town. We don't want to get into bed with out-of-town conglomerates like that," Wes replied.

"How do you figure it would be bad for business?" Vladdy asked.

Wes looked nervous. In the past, he had done nothing but nod his head and agree to whatever it was Dustin or Vladdy was saying. "Here's how much we bring in through tourism," he said pointing at a figure that was scratched on a piece of paper.

Vladdy pulled out figures of his own and explained why the deal would make the town more money and how it would create jobs while residents would still get to enjoy beautiful sections of the park. Dustin and Casper stood back like the heavyweight fighters at a primetime event waiting for the opening match to conclude. After more bickering back and forth between Wes and Vladdy, Dustin finally interjected.

"Look, what's really going on here guys? The deal makes sense for all parties. We will, of course, take care of you guys financially for helping us out on this. We always do."

Wes looked over at Casper unsure of how to proceed. Casper jumped in.

"You know I have great respect for you, Daddy Long Tongue. I'd like to help you out, I really would, but it's election time and the core of my voters won't support this. The woman running against me is pro-environment, family, and town spirit and is starting to gain some traction. It wouldn't be smart for me politically. And if I'm not in office, that's not doing either of us good."

Vladdy glanced at Dustin before saying, "What if we made a healthy donation to your campaign fund? With the extra money we'd be willing to put in, I'm sure you could overcome any difficulties that could arise over this one issue. What do you say?"

"No can-do fellas. I apologize, I wish there were a way we could make it work, but we can't. Not this time."

Dustin and Vladdy walked back to the car in silence. Each of them seemed a little surprised the meeting went the way it did. It appeared as though Pauric had dozed off in the car. As the door opened, he jolted forward and tried to play it off like he had been awake the whole time, even as he was wiping a thick glob of drool off his chin.

"Pauric," Dustin began, "It looks like you will be getting involved in this project after all."

Chapter 23

Mr. Ruggles was in the back office going over the numbers from his first week with Donuts on Blanch open. He had outperformed 10-fold what he originally projected. Already, he had hired another cashier and second cook to relieve Jason and Mathieu of the long hours they were working. Mr. Ruggles could see himself hiring an assistant manager to keep an eye on operations once they grew a little more. Afterall, he had several other businesses to maintain. Perhaps Jason Alfonso would grow into the role. He was familiar with the operation and seemed like a bright young lizard keen to grow his professional career, as well as his paycheck.

Pauric would be making the weekly rounds this morning across Scalestown to collect on Daddy Long Tongue's behalf. The wad of cash Mr. Ruggles was going to give Pauric was going to make him look more dumbfounded than normal. The plan was for Mr. Ruggles to pay his tax to Pauric and then wait until the early evening to pay Dustin a visit. He was hoping that the amount of money Pauric returned with would put Dustin in a good mood and have him eager to learn more about how Donuts on Blanch was already so profitable. It was at this time that Mr. Ruggles would make his case to stick with Glaze Haze instead of switching to Haverfords.

There was a knock at the door. Mr. Ruggles got up and opened it. As predicted, Pauric's ugly mug was looking back at him. In the background, Mr. Ruggles could see Jason trying to duck behind the register to avoid Pauric's gaze.

"Mr. Ruggles," Pauric said gruffly as he side-stepped and entered the office uninvited. "Here's the percentage you owe this week. If you can't pay it all now, you can pay a portion and owe the rest, but remember that there will be interest on that."

Pauric, per usual, sounded rehearsed. Vladdy, no doubt, wrote him a script way back when and Pauric has been reciting it to intimidated business owners across Scalestown ever since. Without skipping a beat, or pausing to say hello, Mr. Ruggles reached into the desk drawer and handed Pauric the envelope. Pauric opened it up and counted the cash. As predicted, he looked surprised at how much had been crammed inside. Pauric thanked him with an expressionless nod and a grunt, pulled the office door open and walked out. Mr. Ruggles saw him blow Jason an overdramatic kiss with a giant grin on his face. Jason readjusted his eyes as if he had been focused intensely on reading the menu above Pauric's head and pretended he hadn't noticed. Based on the deep shade his face blushed, Mr. Ruggles could tell Jason most certainly had noticed. Poor lad.

Chapter 24

Jason was thrown off seeing Pauric and had started to sweat under his arms. He better get used to it, he supposed, as it seemed like it would be a weekly occurrence. The first week had been a whirlwind with a lot of hours worked. Mr. Ruggles had given him and Mathieu an extra bonus to show his appreciation. It was quite the unexpected surprise. Based on the bonus amount, the successful partnering with other Scalestown entities, and the long line of eager faces that stared longingly across the counter at him every day, Jason assumed Donuts on Blanch was off to a better start than his boss had predicted. Jason heard his name being called from the back office. He stuffed a last bite of his donut in his mouth and hopped over the counter to head in that direction.

"Jason my boy. Good morning, I hadn't even realized you were in yet. Sorry that you had to see that unpleasant ogre this early in the morning. I'm sure it's not fun for you."

"No, I can't say that it is," Jason replied, doing his best to force a smile.

"Right, right of course not. How did things go at Temple?" Mr. Ruggles asked.

Jason, now genuinely smiling, replied, "Marvin Deholmes asked for forty boxes a week. He seemed quite impressed"

"Excellent, well done Jason, well done indeed. Our business is in a fantastic position to thrive and you're playing an integral role." Mr. Ruggles was beaming.

The rest of the day flew by for Jason. Another hectic morning, followed by a busy afternoon, and capped off with a chaotic evening. Another day of donuts for breakfast, lunch and dinner. Another day of not wanting to go home where he knew Cassidy was waiting. She had probably been looking up college courses he should be taking and would try to subtly weave it into their conversation, but, per usual, her message would anything but subtle. Jason said goodnight to Mathieu, hung up his apron, took a donut to go, and opened the door for his journey home.

Chapter 25

Wes Helmstead and Casper Fitzpatrick lived four streets away from each other on the east side of town. That would make things easier logistically. Dustin was going to remind both of them who was in charge of this town, regardless of whose names were on the ballot. Vladdy was in the driver's seat singing along lightly to the radio. Dustin was in the passenger's seat. Mr. Ruggles had called earlier wanting to stop by to talk, but Dustin had to push him off until the next night. Tonight's business was more pressing than whatever Mr. Ruggles had on his mind. Pauric was lying on his back under the front of Helmstead's car putting the finishing touches on an explosive device. They had just come from doing the same thing at Fitzpatrick's home. Pauric finished the installation and picked himself up while wiping sweat off his forehead. The dirt and grease caked onto his hand made it worse, but Pauric didn't notice. He lumbered into the backseat. Dustin handed him the detonating device and nodded. Pauric pushed the button and Helmstead's car erupted into a ball of flames. Dustin now looked at Vladdy and nodded his head. Vladdy put the car in drive and pressed the gas to coast away from the scene. They drove the four streets past the Fitzpatrick's. As they were passing the mailbox, Pauric hit the button and Casper's car roared up in flames and smoke. Vladdy kept driving without slowing down, took a left at the end of the street and continued to Dustin's house.

Dustin stepped out of the car. "Nicely done tonight, gentlemen. Pick me up at nine tomorrow morning, and we'll go pay our friends at City Hall another visit." Dustin was confident the message would be received loud and clear.

Pauric was right on time the next morning. Vladdy stepped out of the passenger's seat and moved to the back so Dustin could sit up front. He handed Dustin a copy of the *Lizard Daily*. On the front page, under the fold, was a picture of a burning car. The article reported that two city officials both had car damage the night before. Their friend and author of the article, Beverly Lowery, left out any commentary that foul play might have been involved. Instead it was positioned as an odd and unfortunate coincidence.

"Good," Dustin said. "This means they already know it happened to both of them."

"My guess is Wes ran over to Casper's office this morning in a panic. If it weren't for Casper, he would have gone along with whatever we asked," Vladdy chimed in.

"You want me staying in the car for this one, boss?" Pauric asked.

"No, Pauric. I think it's best if you joined us this time around," Dustin replied. The car pulled up to the far side of City Hall where Casper's office was.

The three lizards got out of the car and closed their respective doors in perfect unison. They walked through the entrance straight past the receptionist without so much as a nod. They didn't knock; Dustin turned the handle and walked into Casper's chamber. Wes and Casper's heads snapped up in a mix of surprise and fear. It was obvious that they had just been talking about last night's events and even possibly arguing about the best way to handle the situation.

"I was wondering if you two had thought any further about our business proposal?" Dustin asked while looking around taking stock of the room.

"Who the hell do you think you are? Was that you last night with the cars? Or your goon over there?" Casper ranted, nodding in Pauric's direction. He continued, "I'm a City Counselor not some small business owner you can push around."

In the background, Wes looked like he was on the verge of being ill. He wanted nothing to do with the situation. Vladdy was right, if not for Casper he'd sign those permits right then and there.

"Have you thought the proposal over?" Dustin asked again, calmly. After all, Casper hadn't answered the question the first time around.

"No, I haven't, and I won't. Get the hell out of my office." Casper said. While he tried to stay confident, his voice waivered slightly as he made eye contact with Pauric.

Pauric's punch was lightning fast. He hit Casper square in the gut. Casper doubled over and clutched his stomach letting out a moan of pain. Pauric grabbed him by the back of the shirt and threw him across his desk. Pens, pads of paper, a stapler, and Casper's body came crashing to the floor. Pauric turned and rounded on Wes.

"No, no, please. I'm on your side here. It's a great deal. I want to sign it," Wes yelled out. Pauric grabbed him by the collar, lifted him several feet off the ground, and pinned him against the wall. He glanced over at Dustin to see what should happen next. A soldier waiting for orders. Dustin shook his head, no. Pauric dropped him and Wes crumpled to the floor and rolled up in a protective ball.

Casper was using the desk to try to prop himself back up to his feet. Dustin reached into his belt and pulled out a gun. He delivered a knee to the same spot in the stomach that Pauric had hit initially. Casper doubled over and was sent back to the floor wheezing. Dustin sat in Casper's leather chair and pulled the lizard's hair back. It was thinning in the back and was sticky with blood. Dustin placed the barrel of the pistol on the bridge of Casper's snout.

"Wes signs today. You bring to your fellow city council members and get it approved. If it's not approved by the end of tomorrow, it's your house that blows up this time."

Casper was breathing hard. "City Council doesn't work that quickly. I won't be able to get this voted on by tomorrow night."

Dustin replied, "You're not a small business owner that gets pushed around. You're an important guy, remember? Surely a lizard of your stature can get a simple task like holding a city council vote done in 24 hours. If you get pushback around kids not having a place to play, let your fellow council members know there is a private donor willing to pay for a new playground so the children can still have fun in a safe place."

Pauric delivered one more blow to the ribs with his giant foot. Dustin reached into his jacket pocket and pulled out an envelope with a stack of cash and tossed it on the floor in between the two men lying on the ground. Better to provide them a taste of the positives they could get out of this than purely operating based on fear. The three of them exited the office.

Chapter 26

The following evening Mr. Ruggles was placing some documents into a beige folder. He had left Donuts on Blanch a little earlier than normal to get home in time to get changed and gather his things before his meeting with Dustin. He had left Jason in charge; he was starting to trust the boy more and more each day.

Mr. Ruggles had changed out of the clothes he had been wearing around the shop all day into a crisp navy-blue suit with polished silver cufflinks. No tie—he wanted to look professional but not like an out-of-touch old lizard unfamiliar with the current trends. He had spent time pulling together information ahead of the meeting. This wasn't going to be Mr. Ruggles on his hands and knees begging for a favor. He had pulled together earnings, new partnerships, the cost of using Glaze Haze, other overhead costs like rent, heat, repairs, etc., and projected sales over the next twelve months. The suit and carefully pulled numbers were in part because Mr. Ruggles knew Vladdy would be at the meeting. Given his business savvy, he was hoping Vladdy could be swayed to provide a rational, unbiased opinion. Mr. Ruggles packed his belongings and headed out to his car to venture over to Dustin's command center.

He hated driving in a suit. The seat belt would get caught up under the top of his jacket and tighten around the upper half of his chest. When he leaned forward to try to create more space, it would automatically tighten with the intention of protecting him against sudden impact. The buckle dug into the side of his shirt, no doubt wrinkling the carefully creased edges. He felt trapped driving in a car, much like he felt trapped working with Dustin.

Chapter 27

Jason had just finished entering money into the register when his phone rang. Cassidy's name appeared on the screen along with a picture of them smiling on a picnic some time last year. Jason realized that he hadn't told Cassidy he was staying late to close up shop.

"Hey Cass. Completely forgot to tell you that Mr. Ruggles asked me to close up shop tonight, so I'll be home later than I originally thought—sorry."

"This is getting ridiculous. We need to talk later. I am not happy," she replied.

Maybe this would be the end of their relationship—and maybe that would be for the best. He knew it was mostly his fault. He hadn't put in the necessary effort to maintain a healthy relationship.

Chapter 28

Mr. Ruggles sighed in relief to see that Vladdy was in fact present for the meeting. He wasn't disappointed that Pauric hadn't been spotted yet either.

"Gentlemen. Thanks for seeing me. How are things?" Mr. Ruggles asked.

"Good evening Mr. Ruggles. We're good," Dustin answered for both of them. "Apologies for having to reschedule from last night; we had a meeting come up last minute that we needed to attend."

"Quite alright, quite alright. I understand how these things go," Mr. Ruggles said, nodding in agreement.

"What can we do for you?"

"As I'm sure you've already heard," Mr. Ruggles began, "Donuts on Blanch is off to a blistering start. I believe a large reason why is because of the quality product that Glaze Haze provides. I brought some information that I'd like to look through with you to see if we can work out keeping them on as a partner."

There was a pause. Dustin appeared to be gathering his thoughts. "So, by 'keeping them on as a partner' are you implying to cut Haverfords out of the deal? Because if that's the case, I think I already made my stance pretty clear."

"Please, Dusti—Daddy Long Tongue," Mr. Ruggles said, catching himself. While he was probably the only living lizard on the planet who could use Dustin's birth-name, he knew he was supposed to avoid doing so in front of others. "Take a look at the data I pulled together."

Dustin shrugged and reached his hand out to accept the documents. Vladdy walked across the room to look over his shoulder. Mr. Ruggles began to narrate his points while the two of them read but Dustin waved his hand shaking him off. Mr. Ruggles stopped speaking. He had been hoping to hold Dustin's hand as he walked him through the documents. Apparently, that would not be the case. Dustin's face remained expressionless, per usual. Mr. Ruggles was pleased to see that Vladdy's expression was indicating that he was impressed with the results from Donuts on Blanch, and to Mr. Ruggles delight, perhaps impressed with Mr. Ruggles himself.

"Congratulations on your early success Mr. Ruggles. These numbers are indeed very impressive. My answer is still no. The opportunity to work with Haverfords on ventures in the future is too great to jeopardize over donuts." Dustin's response was succinct and did not leave any room for misinterpretation.

Mr. Ruggles glanced over at Vladdy. Vladdy looked like he wanted to say something but wasn't going to contradict his boss in front of Mr. Ruggles.

"Will that be all, Mr. Ruggles?" Dustin asked.

"Yes, I suppose it will," Mr. Ruggles said. He knew better than to continue to try to plead his case. He'd have to try to cook up another plan. "Gentlemen," Mr. Ruggles said as he bid farewell.

Chapter 29

Jason grabbed a blanket and pillow and tried to get comfortable on the couch. Cassidy had made an ultimatum—either you're all in or you're out. Before Jason could reply, she told him to think it through carefully and also broke the news that he would be sleeping on the couch that evening. Jason's mind was racing as he was weighing his options. He figured it would be a sleepless night— a lumpy sofa, thin pillow, scratchy blanket and serious life decisions to make. Before he could think about it any further, he dozed off into a comfortable sleep.

Chapter 30

Across town, Mr. Ruggles was sitting in his armchair weighing his options. He had already ignored one phone call from Karim and didn't intend to answer the second if his phone did in fact start buzzing again. In two days, he'd be out of Glaze Haze product and Haverfords would be up and running and ready to deliver a fresh batch. Mr. Ruggles was hoping he'd be able to keep his reputation with Glaze Haze intact, but that did not seem to be in the cards.

Chapter 31

The following afternoon Dustin got a call from Vladdy. Vladdy had gotten word that there was an impromptu City Council meeting being held that night at 7pm, although the agenda for the meeting was not known. Apparently, their visit had been effective. Now they'd have to wait and see if he could get the vote passed. Dustin decided he'd send Pauric to sit silently in the back row. Pauric's figure should stand out enough for Casper and Wes to notice he was in attendance and remember what was at stake. He had Vladdy call Pauric and tell him to attend the meeting, sit in the back row, say nothing to anyone, and take notes on what happened.

Chapter 32

Jason bent down and examined the brick and the glass that was scattered helplessly around it. He picked it up to inspect it closer—a dark red with a combination of grass and mud clinging for dear life to the bottom. It seemed like it could have been plucked right off the walkway that cut across Doris Avenue. Jason pictured an angry lizard, with eyes bulging with rage and tattoos littered across his muscular arms, ripping the brick from its rightful home, getting in his car, and driving to Blanch Street. Jason pictured this fictional lizard kicking the car door open and swinging a giant foot out with the speed and ferocity of a ninja slicing its sword through the antagonist in one of the novels at the Scalestown Library that Jason read as a child. This lizard would have then grabbed the brick off the passenger's seat. There must have been trails of dirt across the seats and center console from the bottom of the brick. A clump of the dirt must have somehow sensed the danger and leapt to safety. It would risk the fate of being absorbed by a vacuum cleaner over what was about to happen next. This lizard, with all his might, would have wound up and thrown the brick through the window of Donuts on Blanch. He must have put his full force behind the throw—closed his eyes and heaved it into orbit with the hopes that gravity would do its job and pull it directly towards his target. Jason pictured the glass shattering, the sound it made, and the silent cheer that muscular lizard must have suppressed when he hit his mark.

It had been two weeks since they had run out of Glaze Haze and had to switch to Haverfords' product. Mr. Ruggles had called Jason and Mathieu to the back room after close the night before they were due to run out. He told them that there was a problem with the supplier and that we'd have to switch in the short term because of their errors. Jason had to divert his eyes to a smudge on the table as he remembered Mr. Ruggles being forced to call Karim to cancel the deal with Glaze Haze. Neither Jason nor Mathieu had thought it would be a big deal. Mathieu was an excellent pastry chef, after all. The first morning with the new Haverfords product, Jason showed up to the shop early and, per usual, had not eaten breakfast before his shift. Now that he had moved out of Cassidy's apartment, his cabinets were completely naked. He reached onto the platter of fresh donuts Mathieu had crafted and took a bite. He stopped chewing immediately. Mathieu happened to look up and noticed the expression on Jason's face and looked over in concern. The donut wasn't good. It lacked its normal fluffy texture as well as some of the flavor that had made it the most delicious treat in all of Scalestown. Jason had originally thought no one would notice the difference but, with one bite, knew they were in trouble.

That morning was Jason's most unpleasant one as an employee at Donuts on Blanch. The first customer in line did not even need to look at the menu. Jason recognized him as one of the daily regulars. He swiftly ordered the *Drizzled Delight*—a raised brioche donut, filled with homemade eggnog custard, doused in brown butter icing and drizzled with salted butterscotch. Jason accepted his money while he dug through the cash register for change, already anticipating the backlash. He scribbled down the order and handed it back through the opening to the kitchen to Mathieu. The next three lizards knew exactly what they wanted as well. Two ordered the *Doris' Avenue*—Rich chocolate cake donuts with vanilla bean glaze, nutella, and fresh blackberries. The third ordered Jason's personal favorite *The Vanilla Bean*—vanilla bean cake donut with homemade vanilla bean caramel, candied pecans, and white chocolate drizzle. Mathieu handed all four orders over to Jason a couple of minutes later. Jason noticed a painful disappointment in Mathieu's eyes; an artist who knows he has not delivered his best work. Jason placed the packaged donuts on the counter and called out the order numbers. Two of the lizards took the bags to go and headed straight for the exit. The other two sat down at tables to enjoy their donuts right there in the shop.

Jason allowed his concentration to wander from the lizard at the counter to see what would happen with these first bites. One of the lizard's eyebrows furrowed. He looked up in shock but politely, with some degree of difficulty, swallowed it down. The other lizard made a loud, dramatic noise and spit it out back into the bag. The next lizard at the counter was trying to get Jason's attention, but Jason was watching the unsatisfied customer start to stand out of his chair to approach the counter.

"This tastes like garbage. It must be stale," the lizard said more calmly than Jason had anticipated. "Could I get a new, fresh one?"

"I'm sorry to hear you didn't like it, but I can assure, sir, it is not stale. We make our donuts in real-time as they're ordered," Jason replied.

"Nonsense. Go back and fetch me another."

Jason paused wondering what he should do. He couldn't give out multiple donuts to every unsatisfied customer, but what choice did he have? He turned around and asked Mathieu for another *Drizzled Delight*. Mathieu handed him one back, not looking confident in its quality. Jason extended it over to the upset lizard who ravenously bit into it. Again, he spit it out and now could no longer control his anger.

"This is awful! Did you get a new cook? What's going on here?" he demanded.

"No, we did not." Jason wished Mr. Ruggles had given them a script to answer these types of questions. He felt like a struggling actor wanting to call out 'line?' to the director. "We have the same cook but are...experimenting with some new ingredients," Jason said, trying to keep things positive.

"Well your experiment sucks. I want my money back."

Just then, the two lizards who had taken their donuts to-go came back into the shop. One of them said, "I think there's been a mistake. This does not taste like it normally does."

The unsatisfied lizard at the counter turned and said, "They aren't defective. They don't taste like they normally do because Dr. Donut over here is trying out some idiotic experiment. Give all of us our money back!"

The other lizards cheered in agreement.

"Ok," Jason said. "Of course, I'm sorry you don't like them. I'll pass your feedback along."

Jason reached back into the register and counted out the money he owed each of them and handed it over. He hoped he was doing the right thing. Mr. Ruggles always talked about customer service and being seen in a positive light by the community, but Jason also knew Pauric came around at the same time every week expecting money in an envelope and would not care about excuses. Returning money to customers would not fill that envelope, and Jason was already familiar with what happens when Daddy Long Tongue is upset.

The four lizards took their money. One of them smiled and thanked him, the other three took it out of his hands aggressively while muttering under their breaths. They made comments to the rest of the customers in the long line about how they should leave because the donuts sucked. Jason hoped they would listen. A handful of lizards left their coveted spots in line and headed towards the door, but Jason was disappointed that the vast majority of lizards stayed. They'd rather taste for themselves than risk not getting their donut.

The same exercise continued on loop for the rest of the morning. Lizards showing up excited and leaving disappointed, infuriated, confused, or some combination of the above. By lunchtime, they had only made two sales. They were to two younger lizards who most likely did not comprehend the concept of a refund, so they dumped their donuts in the trashcan on the way out but did not ask for their money back. At 2pm Jason made the decision to flip the 'Open' sign to 'Closed.' He tried Mr. Ruggles' cell phone for about the fifth time that day and finally he answered. Jason explained the situation and asked what he should do. Mr. Ruggles told him to keep the door closed and that he would be down to the store shortly.

"I wasn't sure what to do," Jason told Mr. Ruggles upon his arrival. "Did I screw up?"

Mr. Ruggles took a deep breath, "No, Jason, you made the right decision. It was a smart move."

Jason breathed a sigh of relief.

Mr. Ruggles continued, "We'll keep the store closed for the rest of the day. Mathieu, I know this is not your fault. Please get some extra flavoring and ingredients and test out to see if you can make these things edible."

The next few days had carried on in a similar fashion. Each morning, Jason would try Mathieu's latest attempt to mask the lackluster donuts that had once been divine and, each morning, despite Mathieu's most valiant efforts, nothing changed. Word had started to spread around Scalestown about the decline of Donuts on Blanch. Yet, to Jason's surprise, each morning there had been a full line waiting when the store opened. Many of those that returned day after day were regulars—each morning, no doubt, praying to Meelosh that things would return to normal at Donuts on Blanch. The thought of missing out on a good batch of donuts outweighed the disappointment of yet another poor experience. Each day, customers became increasingly more hostile. A few days later, Pauric had swung through making his weekly rounds. Jason noticed that the normally cool, calm and collected Mr. Ruggles appeared rattled. Perhaps the mound of cash that had accumulated in the back room from their early successes was steadily declining.

Maybe Cassidy had been right, Jason thought to himself after one particularly unpleasant interaction with an overweight lizard who was at his wits end. Maybe he should have gone back to school and gotten a proper education to put himself in a better position to succeed. He could still do it. The idea still seemed unappealing. After moving out of their apartment, he bunked up with his childhood friend, Oliver Bixby. He had to put most of his stuff in Oliver's basement and was sleeping on a couch that had seen much better days. Initially, Jason could breathe easy for the first time in a long time. He no longer dreaded going home. He didn't miss the constant uneasy feeling of waiting for an argument to start. The fact he was happier, despite all that was happening at work while sleeping on a grubby couch, showed him just how toxic his relationship had been. By the second week he started feeling differently. He was easily irritated and had acted uncharacteristically irrational on several occasions. Mostly it was with random strangers on the street, but Jason caught himself lashing out at Oliver once or twice as well over trivial matters. Maybe Cassidy did provide him emotional support that Oliver Bixby couldn't. Maybe it was the job and the uncertainty of what was coming next. Hell, maybe he just needed a good donut.

Chapter 33

Mr. Ruggles walked down Blanch street with a copy of the *Lizard Daily* tucked securely under his arm. He had gotten Jason's message about property damage at the shop. As he got closer, he could see scattered glass on the sidewalk. He peered into his store as he approached and saw Jason examining something. A brick maybe? Yes, it was a brick. The weapon of choice in a crime of aggression against Mr. Ruggles and his institutions. The suspect? Well, it could be any of the hundreds of angry customers across town. They all had a common motive, and some were now deciding to act.

"Hello, Jason," Mr. Ruggles said as he tried to muster up a smile.

"Good morning, sir," Jason said as he tried to lower the brick out of Mr. Ruggles' line of vision as if to protect him from seeing something traumatic.

"Never a dull moment anymore, is there my boy? Go down the street to Carson's Repairs, would you? Ask for Mr. Carson. He's an older lizard but still quite agile and effective with his tool kit. Give him a description of the damage and see when he can get over here to fix it."

"Yes, sir," Jason said with a nod as he turned and headed down the street.

Mr. Ruggles sighed, slapped his copy of the *Lizard Daily* on a table, and walked to the back closet to grab a broom to sweep away the glass from the sidewalk. The last thing he needed was a lawsuit for some kid slicing open their foot on the shards of glass. The fact that he could be the victim of a crime and still be held legally and financially responsible for an injury that resulted from the damages summed up all that was wrong with government these days. That was beside the point, though. Where did Jason keep the broom? Why wouldn't it be on the left side of the closet on a hook designed to hold a broom? Complete and utter incompetence. Ah, there it is. Tossed aside mindlessly. It had sunk to the floor, just like Mr. Ruggles' reputation was starting to sink as an elite businessman in Scalestown. His mind flashed to the headline he had seen on this morning's paper. Don't read it, he had told himself. It will only aggravate you, his mind pleaded. Sweeping could wait, he needed to read the article. What did Beverly Lowery have to say about him?

Donuts on Blanch? No Thanks

On the day of the grand opening of Donuts on Blanch, I asked Mr. Ruggles what he thought about people saying it was a poor decision to his invest in a store that sold donuts. He replied that not only would he prove the doubters wrong, they'd be in line with everyone else waiting for a donut. I admit, I was among the skeptics. For a couple of weeks, business was booming—long lines, loyal customers, and strong partnerships with other local businesses. I, like everyone else, tried a donut and was blown away with how good they were. But over the last two weeks, things have changed. People started complaining about how awful the donuts tasted. I talked to several residents who had been loyal customers that have given up on the donuts. I went by several times and noticed the lines started to shrink until, over the past couple of days, Donuts on Blanch has turned into a ghost town. So, as any good journalist would do, I went in to verify my sources. I walked into the empty store and ordered the same donut I had previously gotten (The Vanilla Bean) and, quite frankly, it stunk. I couldn't even force it down. The young lizard behind the register avoided my gaze—he had clearly grown used to this reaction from unsatisfied customers.

Mr. Ruggles had to take a deep breath to stay calm as he read.

Not only has it impacted the traffic at Donuts on Blanch, it has also negatively affected his partnerships with other institutions around town. Both Buff's Gym and the Temple have canceled their orders from Mr. Ruggles. The only remaining partnerships are with the retirement home and the school system. A source at the retirement home told me they will most likely be canceling as well. The school system, slowed down by the bureaucracy of group decision making, will surely all vote in favor to cancel after what happened at the Temple yesterday afternoon.

Mr. Ruggles shook his head. His conversation with Gary Dupler at Buff's gym three days ago had not gone well. As soon as he saw he had a missed call from Gary, Mr. Ruggles assumed he wanted to cancel their partnership. Still, Mr. Ruggles felt confident that he could convince Gary to stay on board. Looking back, Mr. Ruggles knew he let his emotions get the better of him during the conversation. Declining sales, a souring reputation, and the lingering image of Pauric's large body were weighing on him. Mr. Ruggles tried to explain to Gary that it was a supply chain issue and that he'd have it figured out shortly. When Gary shot him down again, Mr. Ruggles snapped back telling him that once everything was back to normal, not to come back begging to renegotiate a new deal.

That's right, there was a break in at the Temple. Someone shattered a basement window to steal the excess stock of the original donuts that had not yet been served to the congregation. (Since Temple meets once a week, they had not gotten through their entire order yet).

The basement window hadn't been shattered; it was left unlocked and the thief was able to easily open it up. Mr. Ruggles had seen it first-hand when he went over to talk to Marvin Deholmes about what happened. A slight alteration of the details by Beverly to try to make things sound as juicy as possible. Mr. Ruggles had heard a rumor earlier in the afternoon that somewhere in Scalestown the stolen donuts were being sold out of the back of a trunk. A black market for donuts, who would have thought? Mr. Ruggles was proud in a way. Not only was his product worth robbing a place of worship for, customers were paying marked up prices to buy them out of the trunk of a car. Although, that sense of pride did not outweigh the pains of the lost revenue. After having the Temple broken into, Marvin did not want to continue his arrangement with Donuts on Blanch. Mr. Ruggles wouldn't blame him and didn't try to convince him otherwise. Realistically, given how bad the donuts were now, the threat of a future robbery was non-existent.

Beverly was right. It was a matter of time before the retirement home and the school board backed out of their partnerships with Donuts on Blanch as well. Mr. Ruggles had called Karim on his drive back from his meeting with Deholmes and they started laying the groundwork for a plan.

My question is what happened? Why has the quality dropped off so much? Did Mr. Ruggles misplace his recipe book? Was it yet another poor business decision? This journalist will continue to investigate—stay tuned!

As Mr. Ruggles finished the article, his phone started buzzing and Karim's name flashed across the screen. What timing.

"Hello, Karim."

"My friend, we're on for tonight."

Chapter 34

Dustin adjusted the hard hat on his head. It didn't seem necessary as construction was just about completed, but the site supervisor insisted. Dustin had been skeptical when Douglas Trulio had told him the dam would be completed in two weeks, but here it was, almost finalized. Two weeks earlier, he had sent Pauric off to the emergency City Council meeting that Casper was able to pull together on such short notice to vote on the dam proposal. Pauric returned from the meeting twenty minutes later as he proudly announced the proposal had passed. Pauric was also sure to mention, several times, that he thought Wes Helmstead had shit his pants upon seeing him sitting in the back row. Based on their first interaction, Dustin didn't doubt it. He was surprised how quickly the measure had passed though. Casper must have used either blackmail or cash to get the votes on that proposal so swiftly. The news had made the paper the following morning.

FINALLY – City Hall takes measures to stimulate economic growth

Last night, City Counselors passed a measure that could have serious positive impacts on Scalestown's economy for years to come. Too often we've seen these Counselors shy away from making any bold decisions to help the average Scalestown resident. They finally made progress last night by passing the Haverfords water proposal. This deal will generate thousands of dollars in tax revenue for the town as well as create hundreds of jobs for the citizens of Scalestown. The proposal was spearheaded by City Councilman Casper Fitzgerald and quickly got the votes to pass. According to Mr. Fitzgerald, construction could start as early as this week. Hopefully this is a sign of things to come from our City Counsel.

Dustin had smiled to himself while reading the article. It was certainly worth it to have Beverly Lowery on the payroll to make sure articles like this were reported the way he wanted them to be. The article highlighted the positives of the deal and left out anything negative around out-of-town corporations, taking up tourism revenue, or depriving Scalestown youth from enjoying the great outdoors. Beverly had been pretty harsh towards Mr. Ruggles though, Dustin thought to himself. Was he being too harsh himself? Perhaps, but that didn't change any of Dustin's short-term plans. After finishing the article and his cup of coffee, Dustin was picked up by Vladdy to go meet with Douglas Trulio. When they got to Haverfords headquarters, Trulio was standing in his office with a bottle of champagne and a copy of the *Lizard Daily* on his desk. As they approached, he broke into a slow, dramatic round of applause with an impressed look upon his face. If there had been any doubt about Dustin's pull in Scalestown, there was not anymore. Douglas had handed Dustin and Vladdy each a cigar but did not offer one to Pauric. He pulled out a lighter and extended it so Dustin and Vladdy could light theirs. Douglas proceeded to tell the trio that Haverfords planned on breaking ground on the dam the following morning and was putting an aggressive target of a two-week completion time. He assured them that it was attainable.

Since that meeting smoking cigars with Douglas Trulio, Dustin had remained pretty hands-off with the project. He let Vladdy run with the logistics as well as checking on the progress and working directly with Douglas and the Haverfords team. As he continued to fiddle with his hardhat to get it to sit somewhat comfortably on his head, Dustin took in the progress that had been made over those past two weeks. He was surprised and pleased at what he was now seeing.

The structure looked sturdy and like it would have no difficulty keeping the water split into two sections. It looked like Douglas was going to deliver on his timeline.

Chapter 35

J ason returned to Donuts on Blanch with Buzz Carson as Mr. Ruggles had requested. It did not look like Mr. Ruggles had made any progress on sweeping the glass. Jason glanced inside and saw Mr. Ruggles wrapping up a phone conversation. Buzz Carson set his antiquated toolbox down on the sidewalk and started to examine the damage. Mr. Ruggles came outside and handed Jason the broom.

"Buzz, great to see you. Is this something you can get fixed today?" Mr. Ruggles asked.

Without waiting for a reply from Buzz Carson, Mr. Ruggles handed Jason the broom and asked if he could clean up the glass on the street. He wasn't feeling well and wanted to head home to lie down. Jason, of course, agreed to do the sweeping. Mr. Ruggles turned on his way out and reminded Jason to hang the broom on the hooks on the inside of the closet. They were designed specifically to hold a broom, after all.

Chapter 36

Mr. Ruggles was indeed heading home to rest, but it was not because he was unwell. He'd be out late tonight and was no longer a young lizard who could run on pure adrenaline alone. He now required naps and coffee to function properly after his typical bedtime. Mr. Ruggles was tired of sitting back passively while his business and reputation crumbled. Clearly, he was not going to get any form of support from Dustin and, equally as clearly, Mathieu could not produce a quality donut without using Glaze Haze. Haverfords should stick to its other lines of business and not pretend to be able to produce food ingredients. Mr. Ruggles had called Karim and let him know he was ready to take serious action. Karim couldn't have been happier. His idea was to burn the Haverfords manufacturing plant to the ground. He suggested it so quickly that Mr. Ruggles knew he must have been thinking about it for weeks. It would halt production, but it would also be an incredibly risky move that could have serious repercussions. Karim had assured Mr. Ruggles that it would work. He knew a guy—Scales he called him. Scales had pulled several similar jobs, largely involving insurance scams and Karim claimed he never left a trace. Karim even offered to put the money up for the job himself. They had ironed out all the details, and Mr. Ruggles had to admit it was a pretty solid plan. He told Karim he would think it over. As soon as he had gotten the call from Jason about the brick smashing through his store's window, he called Karim to see if they could kick the plan into action. Mr. Ruggles got home and laid down to rest his eyes. Karim would be picking him up at midnight.

Chapter 37

Jason finished cleaning up the glass and Buzz Carson was getting close to finishing with the window. Out of the corner of his eye, Jason could see an extremely thin lizard speed walking towards him. As he got closer, Jason realized he had his hood up and sunglasses on even though it was not particularly sunny out. The thin lizard reached out his lanky arms and pinned Jason against the side of Donuts on Blanch with surprising strength.

"What the hell?" Jason shouted, feeling the rage boil up inside him. "What are you doing?"

"Give me the good stuff." The lizard spoke frantically while looking over his shoulders as he threatened Jason.

Buzz Carson walked over to try to break it up. The thin lizard took his hands off of Jason to signal to Buzz to back off and mind his own business. That was all Jason needed. He shoved his knee as hard as he could into the lizard's stomach. The lizard buckled over gasping for breath. Something inside Jason snapped. These past few weeks of frustration and irritation at life bubbled to the surface. He found himself pummeling this lizard. One or two shots were probably called for in the name of self-defense. But it quickly passed that point. Jason had him pinned down against the cement delivering blow after blow. Buzz was now trying to pull Jason off the thin lizard. Jason turned around and struck Buzz square in the jaw. Crap, Jason thought to himself. Unsure of what to do, he got up and sprinted away leaving the thin lizard motionless and Babb Carson moaning in pain on the sidewalk.

Chapter 38

Karim showed up a few minutes after midnight. Being even a few minutes late did not help put Mr. Ruggles' nerves at ease. He noticed that it was not Karim's car, yet Karim was in the driver's seat. It must be to avoid anyone recognizing them. In the passenger's seat sat another lizard. This must be "Scales." Mr. Ruggles hadn't caught his actual name and didn't care to. He took a deep breath and started walking towards the car, already having second thoughts. Sure, he had been involved in his fair share of illicit activities but nothing of this nature. As he got into the car, Karim was his normal good-natured self. They could be heading to a bar to have a few drinks for all an outside observer would be able to tell. Scales, however, sat silently in the front seat. Karim gave an enthusiastic introduction to the two lizards, but Scales and Mr. Ruggles didn't exchange a word—just a quick, firm handshake.

"So, let's talk about how this is going to go down," Karim said in a nonchalant tone.

Chapter 39

J ason had retreated to Oliver's apartment where he sat in the bathroom in disbelief over what just happened. He stood up and decided he was leaving to make three stops. The first would be to Buzz Carson's to apologize and offer to pay for any doctor's bills. How he'd be able to pay for that, he was not sure. The second would be to Wild Wilma's for a quick shot of whiskey to calm his nerves. The third and final would be to the Scalestown police department to turn himself in. He was certain the police would end up at his doorstep at some point to arrest him, and the guilt of the incident was driving him crazy.

Chapter 40

Dustin and Vladdy sat in a side booth at Wild Wilma's secluded from the rest of the bar. Dustin was still nursing his first drink as he was planning on volunteering again early in the morning. Three or four times a week, Dustin was making his way to a youth center to volunteer with young kids who didn't have great situations at home. Dustin cared about the children and could relate to not having parental figures in his life at a crucial age. He was planning on making a large donation to build a gym over the course of the next month or so. As rewarding and fun as it could be, Dustin didn't need to show up with a headache. Vladdy was drinking at a faster pace without any obligations the next morning. Dustin was proud of his number two and was glad to see him enjoying himself.

"You've done great with this whole project, Vladdy. You're going to help us make a lot of money. Well done," Dustin said.

Vladdy beamed. Dustin wasn't sure if it was because of the excessive drinking or because of the praise. "Thanks boss. I appreciate the opportunity to run point on this one."

Out of the corner of his eye, Dustin saw the young cashier that worked for Mr. Ruggles walk into the bar. What was his name? Dustin couldn't remember. It looked like he had healed up ok from the beating Pauric had laid on him. Dustin watched the cashier order a shot of whiskey, knock it back like it was water, and immediately order another. Perhaps he had healed up physically but not mentally.

Dustin called the waiter over and pointed at Mr. Ruggles' cashier and instructed him to let the boy know his bill had been paid for. Dustin watched as the waiter walked over and talked to the bartender. The bartender then walked over to Mr. Ruggles' cashier and pointed towards Dustin's booth as he explained the bill had already been paid. The young cashier glanced over with a mix of surprise and curiosity. Upon seeing Dustin and Vladdy, the color drained out of his face. He gave a quick, awkward wave of appreciation, gathered his jacket, and scurried out of the bar without a second glance at anyone.

Chapter 41

Jason hurried towards Wild Wilma's exit and pushed the door open as quickly as he could. Shit, just what he needed—a Daddy Long Tongue sighting. Why the hell had he bought his drinks? At least Pauric hadn't been with them. Jason began his walk over to the police department. He hadn't had the courage to walk up Buzz Carson's driveway to apologize face-to-face. He'd do it after turning himself in. By the time Jason started making his way up the steps to the station, the couple of whiskey shots were starting to sink in, giving him the confidence he needed to confess his sins. He walked in and was greeted by a middle-aged officer. The station was surprisingly warm and welcoming with a hint of a smell of stale take-out food in the air. Jason took a deep breath and explained what happened. The officer seemed to appreciate that he had turned himself in but also couldn't hide a hint of disgust that he was the one who had inflicted harm on poor Mr. Carson. The officer told him he could make a phone call. Jason racked his brain on who he could call. His immediate reaction was Cassidy. But, no, that was out of the question. Oliver, maybe? No, what help would Oliver be. Jason sighed and realized his best bet was Mr. Ruggles. He took his time to punch in his number. His stomach was starting to hurt as the line was ringing on the other end. Was it the whiskey or the nerves? Probably a combination of both, Jason thought to himself. Five rings, six rings, seven rings and then the familiar sound of Mr. Ruggles voice came through over voicemail. Jason left a short vague message telling his boss that he was at the police station and was making his one phone call and asked him to call back into the station when he got the chance. The officer shrugged after seeing that Jason couldn't get through to whoever he had contacted.

"You'll have to stay the night and you can try to make a call again in the morning," the officer told him.

Chapter 42

As Karim was outlining his plan in the car, Mr. Ruggles could feel his phone buzzing in his pocket. He pulled the tip out to get a glance at who the call was from. It was from a number he did not recognize. He shoved it back into his pocket—now was not the time to get distracted. The car pulled down the street that the Haverfords plant was located on. The plan was for Scales to slip out of the car undetected and for Karim and Mr. Ruggles to pick him up around the back side of the building. Mr. Ruggles gave the 'OK' on the plan, mainly because he knew he was out of his element here. As the car slowed to a stop, Scales opened the door and silently exited. As he did, his jacket got caught on the seatbelt for a split second. From the backseat, Mr. Ruggles got a glimpse of a stockpile of what looked like explosive devices stashed inside. As soon as the door closed, Karim pulled slowly away from the curb to circle around the back of the building.

Mr. Ruggles was sweating through his shirt in the backseat. Karim had parked the car at the back of the building and was humming a song under his breath. There was no sign of Scales.

"Is this supposed to be taking this long?" Mr. Ruggles asked, trying to sound composed.

"Yes, my friend. He needs to set the explosives in a specific spot so that it looks like it could have been a gas leak that caused the fire. Scales is a pro. He should be walking out in the next two minutes."

Karim stopped short as he peered off into the distance. Mr. Ruggles had seen it too. There was movement about forty yards away from them by the exit, and it was not Scales.

"Shit," Karim said, for the first time showing concern. "It's a security guard."

"I thought you said there would be no security here?" Mr. Ruggles said in a panic, no longer trying to hide his fear.

The security guard must have heard some noise from the building. He now had his weapon drawn. Karim turned on the engine and accelerated towards the guard. The engine groaned trying to muscle the power Karim's foot was demanding of it.

"What are you doing?" Mr. Ruggles shouted.

A loud crack and a spray of glass, followed by another. The guard had deduced that the oncoming vehicle was hostile and fired two rounds from his pistol. Neither shot appeared to have hit Karim. Mr. Ruggles could see the look of realization in the security guard's eyes that he had not hit his mark and that the car was still coming at him just as ferociously. In another instant, there was a sickening crunch as the car struck the guard with full force. Leaving the engine running, Karim kicked the door open and scurried out. The guard was trying desperately to crawl away. With zero hesitation, Karim reached into the back of his pants and brandished his own firearm. One pull of the trigger, and a bullet went through the back of the guard's head. He now laid still. Karim looked up and raised his weapon as he heard fast approaching footsteps but saw it was Scales.

Scales, still showing no emotion, simply said, "We need to get the body into the trunk."

Karim got out of the car to help Scales with the body. He turned towards Mr. Ruggles and said, "Ruggles get behind the wheel and be ready to floor it." For the first time, Mr. Ruggles did not demand that someone call him 'Mr.'

Arms and legs shaking, Mr. Ruggles did as he was told. He watched Karim and Scales pick the body up and try to get it to fit in the trunk. After they managed to do so, they both jumped in the back seat and Mr. Ruggles stepped on the gas with all his might. As the car pulled down the road there was a massive explosion. Mr. Ruggles could see a burst of flame high above the tree line in his review mirror. Karim started chuckling to himself while letting out a string of curse words under his breath.

"What now?" Mr. Ruggles asked while trying to focus on his breathing to make sure he didn't pass out behind the wheel.

"First off, slow down. Go the speed limit. Second, we need to get rid of this car," Scales said before Karim had the chance to answer. "Karim, you have a friend down at the scrapyard, right? Can they take care of the body, too?"

"Yes," Karim replied.

"Good. Call and arrange getting this car destroyed. Tonight. Drop Mr. Ruggles off at home and me off at my car. I'll follow you over to the scrapyard to give you a ride back home," Scales replied.

Karim nodded and took out his phone to make the call. For the first time, Scales smiled and said, "Mr. Ruggles, my rate just increased."

It was Mr. Ruggles' turn to nod. He would pay this maniac whatever he wanted if they got out of this situation unscathed.

Chapter 43

Mr. Ruggles woke up to his phone ringing. He fumbled to try to take it off the charger. He looked and saw that it was the same number that had called the night before. Mr. Ruggles cleared his throat and answered the phone, trying to sound alert and confident.

"Hello?" he asked.

"Mr. Ruggles?" the unknown voice replied.

"Yes, who is this?"

"This is Detective Avery from the Scalestown Police Department."

Mr. Ruggles felt dizzy. Had they already been caught? What did Karim and Scales do with the car? He mustered up the courage to reply, "Hello, Detective. What can I do for you?"

"You don't know what this is about?" Detective Avery asked back.

Shit shit shit shit. "No, I do not."

"Oh, well I guess you haven't checked your voicemail. Not an issue. Last night, a lizard named Jason Alfonso came into the station and turned himself in for an assault outside of your store. He claims to work for you and chose you to be his one phone call."

"Sweet Meelosh. What happened?" Mr. Ruggles replied with a mix of concern for Jason and relief for himself.

"He got threatened outside of your store and fought back with, shall we say, excessive force. He also struck an older man who had been fixing your window."

"Buzz Carson?" Mr. Ruggles asked. This didn't seem like Jason at all. Then again, how well did Mr. Ruggles actually know the young cashier?

"That is correct. We would have tried to get in touch with you a second time last night, but the entire team got pulled down to the fire at Haverfords."

Mr. Ruggles felt dizzy again. He tried to sound as innocent as possible, "What happened at Haverfords."

"I guess you haven't seen the paper yet this morning. Check out the front page—you can't miss it." Mr. Ruggles started walking towards his front door as the Detective continued, "Can you get down here to bail the kid out?"

"Yes, I'll get dressed and be down shortly."

Chapter 44

Dustin had woken up to texts from Vladdy telling him to check the front page of the *Lizard Daily*. Dustin walked downstairs, put on a pot of coffee, and opened the door to his front porch to grab the paper. As he reached down to get it, he saw "Haverfords" in big bold letters. Uh oh.

Explosion at Large Manufacturing Plant

There was a large explosion early Thursday morning at one of Haverfords' large industrial manufacturing plants. Haverfords, for those readers that do not know, entered an agreement with the city to supply surrounding towns with Scalestown's water. According to a Haverfords spokesperson, this plant did not have anything to do with the water treatment equipment. Authorities are still investigating the explosion, but the early signs indicate that it was caused by a gas leak. There are no reported injuries as the building was empty at the time of the explosion. We reached out to Councilman Casper Fitzpatrick for comment but have not received any word back from his office. Mr. Fitzpatrick is the one who pushed the vote through City Council to approve the Haverfords water project.

Dustin placed the newspaper down. He was relieved it had nothing to do with the water operation. He picked up his phone and texted Vladdy back asking what was manufactured at that particular plant. Vladdy replied, "different food products and ingredients. Including materials for donuts…"

Would Mr. Ruggles be this bold and idiotic, Dustin wondered to himself? His shop was hurting financially so it was a possibility. But it seemed like it was out of character and beyond Mr. Ruggles' capabilities.

He looked at his watch and realized that, if he didn't get moving, he would be late getting over to the youth center. The Scalestown Youth Center wasn't anything to write home about. It was an archaic building that was in desperate need of renovations. When you entered, you had to get past Debbie. She was an older lizard who looked as though she had been working there for decades. She wore many hats—part security guard, part secretary, part manager. When a fight broke out, she was chief negotiator and when a piece of sporting equipment went missing, she was lead detective. Dustin was always impressed with her calm, cheerful demeanor despite the surrounding chaos she had to deal with. Pauric would have a hard time getting some of these young lizards to behave, yet, for all of their tough talk, very few ever broke the rules Debbie governed by.

When you got past Debbie, you entered a narrow hallway that split off into three directions. To the left, there was a small room for Arts & Crafts. The supply was rather limited. To create a masterpiece, you'd have to use a random assortment of colored pencils, popsicle sticks, tissue paper, a dull pair of scissors and a dangerous looking hot glue gun. Still, many of the young lizards would spend their time in the Arts & Crafts room. Dustin found himself in there on one of his first days volunteering. A kid asked him for help cutting letters out of paper so he could spell his name and glue them together. Dustin agreed to help, but assembling crafts wasn't a strength of his, and the perplexed look he got from the young lizard when he handed over his finalized product confirmed just that.

Across from the Arts & Crafts room was the toddler section. It was a simple room with a handful of stuffed toys scattered about for the youngest of lizards. There was a picture on the wall, with a sizable crack down the middle, of a young lizard playing in a sandbox. The floor was tile with deep stains and smears that a professional cleaning crew would have trouble waging war against. There was one window, but the view from that window looked out over a vacant alley with an overflowing dumpster. Dustin soon realized he wanted to stay away from the toddler room. The wide array of sounds, smells, and liquids being churned out was overwhelming.

At the far end of the hallway was the basketball court. Here, every single day, is where the utter chaos unfolded. At any given time, the court could be hosting up to four different games. There'd be a basketball game going alongside dodgeball, tag, and a bowling match with a toy set of plastic pins. It was often difficult to distinguish where one activity ended and another started. It was quite common that a lizard running after a basketball would be the one to knock down the pins, instead of the bowling ball itself. The lizards seemed to have adapted to the chaos because there were rarely arguments or conflicts between groups. From what Dustin could tell, it was, overall, a nice group of lizards who just may not have had the support or supervision at home that could keep them out of trouble. Dustin always made sure to leave before parents came to pick their kids up—the last thing he wanted was people thinking he was down there trying to recruit his next batch of soldiers to expand his empire.

The first day Dustin spent volunteering in the back room he was unsure what to do. He didn't want to interject himself into a kid's game if they didn't want an adult playing. After a while, the bowling game needed an extra player, so Dustin was able to interact with some of the young lizards that way. On his next visit, he was called upon to play in one of the basketball games. To start, Dustin wasn't exerting too much effort. Afterall, he was a full-grown lizard, and these were children. He was giving some of the lizards he was covering open shots. This started ticking off some of his own teammates as it was a close game. The lizard

Dustin was covering scored for a second time in a row and started talking some trash. The next possession, the same lizard went up to take a shot and Dustin blocked it as hard as he could. The ball rolled all the way over through the dodgeball game, much to the delight of his teammates. One of Dustin's teammates had to negotiate a cease-fire with the lizards playing dodgeball so he could safely pass through the game to retrieve the basketball. The next possession, Dustin pulled up and shot the ball from two feet behind the three-point line and sunk it to give his team the win. The lizard on the other team who had been trash-talking now had a giant grin on his face and came over to give Dustin a fist-bump. Dustin realized that while the lizards may be young, they had witnessed a lot in their lives that forced them to grow up quickly. On the court, they weren't looking to be coddled—they were looking to compete.

Chapter 45

J ason hadn't slept much. He spent the night in an 8x10 foot jail cell. It was actually more privacy than he had at Oliver's and the cot was just as comfortable as the couch back home. A combination of guilt, uncertainty, and a screaming drunk one cell over kept him awake.

The officer had walked over a few minutes earlier and said that Mr. Ruggles was on his way down to the station. Jason started to get anxious about what to say to his boss. He had told the police he acted in self-defense and accidently struck Buzz Carson in the chaos. Jason left out the part about the unnecessary repeated blows to the attacker's head and mid-section. He hadn't heard how the guy was doing yet. Jason was certain that a doctor would confirm that there was more damage here than a case of self-defense, not to mention Buzz Carson's version of events. The station door opened, and Mr. Ruggles walked in. He walked over to the two officers sitting behind the desk and greeted them both by name while shaking each of their hands enthusiastically. There was some quick dialogue back and forth and then one of the officers pointed over at Jason and started mimicking kicking and punching. Mr. Ruggles shook his head sympathetically and did some talking of his own. Then he reached into his jacket pocket and pulled out an envelope and handed it to one of the officers. The officer tried to position his body to shield the envelope from Jason's gaze, but Jason could tell that the officer was counting through a stack of money. Jason wondered how much money was in the envelope. Did Mr. Ruggles care about him? Or was he just worried about bad publicity? The officer accepted the envelope and shook Mr. Ruggles' hand and walked over to the cell. He sifted through his set of keys until he found the right one. The officer unlocked the door and told Jason he was free to go.

Chapter 46

J ust great, Mr. Ruggles thought to himself as he turned to leave the jail with Jason trailing in his wake. He may soon be in need of some serious favors from the Scalestown police and here he was cashing one in for Jason Alfonso. The truth was, he did care about the boy and did not want to see any harm come to him. He also still felt a sense of guilt for Jason's introduction to Pauric. Not to mention, the last thing Mr. Ruggles needed was any additional negative attention about him coming out. Now was the time to lay in the weeds.

Jason looked defeated. He was skinnier than Mr. Ruggles had noticed in the past. Perhaps he had lost some weight since he and his girlfriend had broken up. Mr. Ruggles had overheard Jason having a private conversation with a friend who stopped in the shop about how things had ended. Mr. Ruggles recalled losing a decent amount of weight himself after losing Darlene.

"I'm so sorry, Mr. Ruggles. I didn't know who else to call. I'm sorry," Jason sounded like he was on the verge of tears. "I was just so angry after someone smashed our window and then some stranger attacking me right outside our entrance. I'll pay you back, I promise."

Mr. Ruggles looked around to make sure no one heard. Jason must have seen the envelope exchange. He motioned for Jason to get into the car. "It was the right move to call me. It's unfortunate that you got attacked. I'm glad you weren't hurt. As for what you witnessed in the station...you can never repeat that to anyone. You don't need to pay me anything. You just owe me your loyalty and hard work."

Jason nodded vigorously. He gave directions to Mr. Ruggles to Oliver's. When the car stopped outside of the apartment, he again expressed his gratitude and appreciation for what Mr. Ruggles had done. Mr. Ruggles smiled and nodded as Jason exited the car. As he was pulling away from the curb, his phone started ringing. It was Dustin's number.

"Hello?" Mr. Ruggles said upon flipping his phone open.

"Good morning, Mr. Ruggles. I'd like to meet. Are you free this afternoon?"

"In regard to what?" Mr. Ruggles asked, perhaps too overanxiously.

"We'll discuss when you're here. See you at 2pm," Dustin said, without waiting for Mr. Ruggles to provide any open time slots.

"Ok, see you then," Mr. Ruggles replied and hung up the phone.

Right after hanging up, he called Karim for a status update. He answered on the fourth ring.

"Good morning, my friend. How are you holding up?" he asked.

"I've felt better. Did you read the paper? Authorities don't suspect foul play," Mr. Ruggles said.

Karim chuckled, "Scales was worth the money then, huh?"

Mr. Ruggles did not chuckle back. "Have you heard anything else on your end about it?"

"Nothing at all. After we dropped you off, things went as planned. Relax, my friend. I think we may be in the clear."

Mr. Ruggles did not relax, but it was at least welcome news that things went smoothly after he had been dropped off. "I just got off the phone with Daddy Long Tongue. He wants to meet this afternoon."

"Oh?" Karim replied.

"I'll use this as an opportunity to get approval to get back to using Glaze Haze. As long as there is nothing linking us to the explosion, I think he'll let us start business back up together."

After a few seconds Karim replied, "Call me when you're done with the meeting."

Mr. Ruggles knocked on Dustin's door. Dustin answered almost immediately and extended his arm to usher Mr. Ruggles inside. Mr. Ruggles looked around and did not see any signs of Vladdy or Pauric.

"Is it just you and I today, Dustin?" Mr. Ruggles asked while craning his neck to try to see in the other room.

"Yes, just the two of us Mr. Ruggles. I need to know right now. No bullshit. Did you have anything to do with this explosion at Haverfords?"

Mr. Ruggles kept his best poker face on. He decided against acting surprised or insulted. "I figured that's why you called me down here. No, Dustin, I had nothing to do with it. The paper said it was a gas leak. I wouldn't even know how to do that if I wanted to."

It's true, Mr. Ruggles thought. Without Karim and Scales, he would never have had a chance pulling off what they did.

Dusting sighed, "Ok. But if I find out otherwise, you'll face the same reckoning any other ordinary lizard would. Understood?"

Mr. Ruggles nodded, "I'd expect nothing less."

Dustin continued, "My guess is you'd like to start using Glaze Haze again now that our supply from Haverfords has been rendered useless?"

"Yes," Mr. Ruggles said. "It can make us both more money, Dustin. Be reasonable. You know this makes the most sense business-wise."

Dustin nodded. He had clearly already given this thought. "Fine. Rekindle your relationship with Glaze Haze. I'm sure that scumbag will be delighted to have you back as a customer." Mr. Ruggles knew he was referencing Karim.

"Ok, thank you, Dustin. Anything else?" Mr. Ruggles asked, attempting to contain his excitement.

"No, that will be all. Get those sales back up so you can keep paying Pauric."

Mr. Ruggles flashed a smile, "That's the plan."

The two lizards shook hands and Mr. Ruggles walked back to his car. Once he got in, he reached for his phone. It slipped out of his hands and fell into the center console. Mr. Ruggles realized how sweaty his hands were as a result from his conversation with Dustin. He dug it out of the cup holder while backing out of the driveway and pulled up Karim's number to give him the good news.

Chapter 47

Dustin watched Mr. Ruggles back out of the driveway. He wasn't sure if he believed him but, regardless, if donut sales started increasing it would put more money in his pockets. If no evidence came out to link Mr. Ruggles to the explosion that would strain his relationship with Haverfords, it might be for the best. Dustin's next call would be to Douglas Trulio—better to get ahead of this than let Douglas' imagination start running wild about a conspiracy theory aimed at taking him down. Before he could make the call, his phone started ringing. Douglas was calling him.

"Good afternoon, Douglas."

"Hello. I assume you saw the news?" Douglas responded.

"Of course. I was actually just taking out my phone to call you. How do the damages look?" Dustin asked.

"We'll lose out on money, of course. But if a building had to be lost, that wasn't an awful one. As I'm sure you're aware from the paper, it won't impact our water treatment project." Douglas continued, "We will no longer be able to provide you with the donut ingredients, however. So, Mr. Ruggles will have to switch up the menu for the foreseeable future."

"Excellent news that it won't disrupt our operation. I gave Mr. Ruggles permission to switch back to his previous supplier so that we can continue operations," Dustin replied.

"You, what? That wasn't part of the agreement," Douglas retorted.

"Douglas, the name of the store is 'Donuts' on Blanch. I'm not going to have him remove donuts from the menu while we wait for your operation to get back up and running. It will be money lost, and that doesn't make any sense."

"He was probably behind it. He was always bitter about the way things turned out with his business. Are you going to stand for that?" Douglas shot back—anger now noticeable in his voice.

Dustin remained calm, "I can assure you that while Mr. Ruggles can be a sly businessman, he is not capable of anything of this nature. Plus, by your own investigation, the explosion was caused by gas leaks. Let's not get hung up on this. The amount of money we are making, and will continue to make, on the water supply makes this insignificant."

"Ok, fine. Fair enough," Douglas said, although he did not sound one hundred percent convinced.

Chapter 48

"We're back on, Karim," Mr. Ruggles said into the phone.

Karim let out a deep guffaw. "You had him wrapping his long tongue right around your nuts, didn't you my friend?"

Mr. Ruggles ignored the comment but couldn't help smirking. He had pulled one over on Daddy Long Tongue, and that was not something a lot of lizards could say. "When can you get our supply dropped off?"

"We can have it over to you by tomorrow morning, my friend."

"Even though it's a Sunday?" Mr. Ruggles asked, in case Karim had lost track of which day of the week it was. He seemed like the type of lizard that lived one day at a time.

"Good business doesn't sleep, does it, Mr. Ruggles?" Karim asked while chuckling.

"I'll have my chef meet your contact at the store in the morning. We'll be up and running for Monday." Mr. Ruggles replied.

"I assume you have a plan to start making our money back?" Karim asked.

"Of course, I do."

This was great news. Mr. Ruggles hadn't expected to be able to get up and running by Monday. His next step would be to call Mathieu and Jason. He wanted Mathieu to come in and start making donuts and Jason to come in to help get things cleaned up and ready to go. He'd also send Jason out to hand out some free samples around town to get the buzz going again. After regaining the trust of the community's taste buds, he would revisit the partners that had canceled on him to get their business back.

Chapter 49

Jason had spent most of the afternoon and early evening wandering around Scalestown. He walked all the way down Doris Avenue and onto a side street that ended up leading to a path in the woods. He strolled through the woods until it brought him to another side street that, after a series of twists and turns, eventually connected with Blanch Street. There was no evidence on the sidewalk outside of Donuts on Blanch to suggest an incident had happened the night before. Jason pulled his hood up and hurried past. He did not feel like going home and having to talk to Oliver or provide a reason for his absence the night before. If Jason gave the same story he had given to the police officers, Oliver would probably eat it up and think he was a bad ass, which is not the way he felt. The idea of feeling admiration was appealing, but it did not outweigh the guilt he knew he'd feel in his stomach upon retelling the tale. Jason figured he'd walk a few more hours and then hope Oliver would be cooped up in his room playing video games allowing Jason to sprawl out on the couch unharmed.

His phone rang. Jason had trouble understanding Mr. Ruggles at first because he was speaking so quickly and excitedly. The call ended with an enthusiastic "good night!" from Mr. Ruggles. Apparently, Jason would need to work this weekend handing out free donuts. It was better than being bored and alone with his own thoughts.

Jason walked up to his apartment and the lights were out. Oliver must have turned in early. Jason fiddled with his keys and tried as quietly as he could to unlock the door without waking him. Before he finished twisting the key into the lock, a light turned on and Oliver swung the door open. The look on his face was a mix of relief and curiosity.

"Dude! Where have you been? Wendell said he saw you walking out of the police station this morning!" Oliver shouted out.

Wendell was a lizard who graduated a year below Jason and Oliver. He was nice enough but wasn't overly sharp. His main claim to fame was that in the ninth grade, during first aid training, he stabbed himself with an epi-pen that he thought was a fake one used for training purposes. Wobbly Wendell, everyone called him after that. Jason was thankful Oliver mentioned that Wendell spotted him leaving the jail early on in the conversation. It would have been embarrassing getting caught in a blatant lie.

"I got jumped outside of the donut shop last night," Jason replied simply.

"Jumped? What do you mean jumped? By who? Why? What happened?" Oliver was having difficulty containing his excitement.

"I don't know. Some skinny lizard I had never seen before. He wanted donuts I think."

"Ok, so he attacked you, what happened next?"

Jason did not want to get into this. "I grabbed him and tossed him to the ground and then got on top of him and punched him a bunch of times."

"Damn good for you. Guy sounds like he got what he deserved. I would have done the same thing," Oliver replied confidently.

Jason doubted Oliver had ever been in any sort of physical altercation in his life. Jason had only been in a couple himself, and they were more like shoving matches resulting from sporting competitions—nothing like this.

Oliver continued, "So, who called the police?"

"I went to the station and turned myself in." Jason was starting to get agitated with the conversation. He just wanted to lay down and shut his eyes.

"What?" Oliver asked flabbergasted. "Why the hell would you do something so stupid?"

Jason didn't want to mention there was a third witness. He did not want Oliver, or anyone for that matter, knowing that he struck Buzz Carson square in the jaw.

When Jason didn't answer, Oliver continued, "That's one of the dumbest things I've ever heard. So, what's your punishment? I never would have turned myself in."

Jason snapped. "You wouldn't have turned yourself in because you would never get into a fight. I don't want to talk about it. Go back to bed, leave me the hell alone."

Oliver looked surprised and somewhat wounded. He nodded his head, mumbled something under his breath and turned around to go back upstairs.

Jason was too annoyed to care about Oliver's feelings. He flopped down on the sofa, kicked his shoes off and closed his eyes. He was so tired that he expected to be able to fall asleep right away. The couch felt less comfortable than the jail bed had the night before, and Jason felt more trapped than when he was locked behind steel bars. At a crossroads with his feelings, Jason decided he'd go to Temple this weekend in search of some spiritual guidance.

Chapter 50

Mr. Ruggles showed up at Donuts on Blanch the following morning feeling better than he had in a long time. Jason and Mathieu were waiting out front for him when he arrived. Not a surprise that Jason had arrived early, given recent events.

"Boys!" Mr. Ruggles exclaimed dramatically. "Today is the day! We're back in business! There will be a delivery truck showing up any minute. When it does, start unloading the ingredients. Mathieu, start cooking as soon as it's unloaded! Jason, stock the shelves, dispose of the garbage, and clean the kitchen. Once we have a big batch made, we'll take to the streets to start handing out free samples."

Mathieu looked energized. The inability to produce a quality product had been weighing on him. Jason probably wasn't excited to be stocking shelves, but he was eager to show his commitment and loyalty to Mr. Ruggles.

"Jason, could you go back to Temple later this morning and drop off a batch for the ceremony? No need to mention anything to Deholmes about payments or contracts. Let's just show some good faith. Get it — faith? You see what I did there, Jason? Of course, you do, you're a sharp kid," Mr. Ruggles rambled on.

"Yes, sir, I can. I was planning on going to Temple anyways. Try to clear my head and what not," Jason replied.

"I'm glad to hear that, Jason," Mr. Ruggles said with a smile. "I'll be in the back getting some affairs in order."

A delivery truck pulled up outside the storefront. "Ah, great timing. As promised boys, as promised."

Without another word, Jason and Mathieu walked out of the store, greeted the driver, and started the unloading process.

Chapter 51

An hour later, Jason's stomach started to grumble with hunger. It was still early, and he hadn't eaten breakfast. Mathieu had retreated to the kitchen to start cooking about thirty minutes earlier. Jason was just about finished getting everything inside the store settled when Mathieu emerged from the kitchen with a child-like grin on his face. He held up a tray of donuts for Jason to see. Jason grinned back and rushed across the room to take a look—these better be good. Mathieu held the platter out and gestured for Jason to help himself. Jason reached out and picked one of the donuts up. It looked like a *Drizzled Delight,* but he couldn't be sure without a tasting. It was every bit as delicious as he remembered. When Jason took the bite, it felt like all the anger, frustration, and irritation he had been feeling washed away. This was as good as he had felt in weeks. Jason's instincts had not betrayed him, it was, in fact, a *Drizzled Delight.* Could this be his new favorite? He broke into a grin himself and gave Mathieu two thumbs up before reaching in and grabbing another donut. Customers would surely be lining up around the corner like they used to once word hit the street that the donuts were back.

Mathieu handed Jason three packaged boxes of donuts and Jason hit the streets ready to canvas the neighborhood to get word out there that Donuts on Blanch was back. Jason first headed to Scalestown Diner. With runny eggs, dry toast and poor service, the diner was never an overly successful place. Donuts on Blanch had pushed it on the verge of going out of business. Since the decline of Donuts on Blanch, some of the older regulars had started going over to the diner for their breakfast, mainly to socialize. Jason walked up and stood outside the front door. He didn't know the name of the grumpy old lizard who served as owner and chef (if you could call him a chef), but Jason could only assume he would not be pleased to see a Donuts on Blanch employee outside his window. A group of older lizards was coming down the street approaching the entrance of the diner. Jason recognized them. They had been regulars at Donuts on Blanch—in fact, one of them had led the revolt against Jason the first day they started getting complaints about Mathieu's creations. They seemed to recognize him too.

"Applying for a new job? Donut shop can't afford to pay you any more with that garbage they're selling?" the ringleader asked.

"Or maybe he's just sick of working for that buffoon Ruggles," a second chimed in, making the ringleader and the third lizard burst out laughing.

"Mr. Ruggles," Jason corrected him. "I've got some good news for you fellas. We're back up and running with the originals. Here, I brought some samples."

Out of the corner of his eye, Jason could see the owner of the diner standing at the door ready to greet his customers and show them to their table.

The three lizards looked at each other, shrugged and each reached in. Upon biting into the donuts, their faces all lit up.

"Sweet Meelosh!" one exclaimed.

"Kid, these are great. Screw this place and their runny eggs!" the ringleader said emphatically.

Jason could practically feel their frustrations wash away with their bites, just as it had done for him. With that, the three lizards turned around and headed in the other direction towards Blanch Street. The owner was looking out suspiciously at Jason wondering what happened to his three potential customers. A few minutes later, more potential diner customers walked up to the door, talked to Jason, and turned on their heels to leave the diner. The owner now popped his head out the door and started yelling at Jason to get the hell off his property. Jason bit into another donut, gave a neighborly wave, and walked away from the diner, smiling.

His next stop was around the back side of the high school where a lot of the more rebellious teenage lizards would hang out. A group of teenagers looked at Jason suspiciously as he walked over towards the bleachers they were sitting on. He offered them each a sample. After trying them, the young lizards all high-fived and left school grounds to walk towards Blanch Street. A custodian came outside and started yelling at the students to get off school property, but they were already out of earshot.

Jason's next stop was the Temple. He was feeling very uncomfortable and was now wondering why he had wanted to come at all. What would Temple offer him now that it hadn't in the past? Besides, things seemed to be back on track with Donuts on Blanch, so perhaps he was just overreacting to one or two bad breaks? The fact that he would most likely run into Cassidy didn't help. He was considering just dropping the donuts off and leaving when he heard a familiar voice call out his name.

"Jason?" It was Cassidy.

"Hey Cassidy. How are you?" he said with an awkward smile.

She ignored the pleasantry. "Here conducting another business deal?" she asked, eying the box of donuts under his arm.

"No. Well, I do have this as a gift for Mr. Deholmes but that's not why I'm here. Well it's part of why I'm here. But I was going to come anyways." Jason stumbled over his words. Seeing her for the first time since their breakup was throwing him off.

Her expression changed, "Why are you here then? Hoping you'd run into me?" she said with a playful smile.

He smiled back, "Just looking for somewhere to reflect and relax."

She nodded but did not ask him to explain further. "Well, I hope you find that here this morning. See you, Jason," she said as she walked away.

Jason waved goodbye. He was a little surprised she didn't invite him to sit with her but, at the same time, was relieved that she hadn't. Jason wandered around looking for Marvin Deholmes until he bumped into him coming out of the restroom.

They made eye contact. Jason could tell the man was trying to place him. Jason walked over and extended his hand.

"Good morning, Mr. Deholmes. I'm Jason Alfonso. I was here a few weeks back with some donuts from Mr. Ruggles. I'm Cassidy's...err...friend."

"Ah, Jason that's right. I'm sorry we haven't seen you around since then," he replied, piously.

"Right. I know, I've been busy." It was all Jason could think to say. When Marvin did not reply, Jason continued, "I have a gift from Mr. Ruggles. He apologizes about the quality of our product over the past few weeks but wanted you to know that we are back to our original donuts. Here, taste one for yourself."

Marvin reached out and tried a donut. His eyes lit up. "Well, I'll be. These are delicious. Knowing Mr. Ruggles, he wants to talk business about getting these back in our Temple?"

"Not that I've heard, sir," Jason replied.

Marvin looked back skeptically. "Well, thank you for dropping them off. Will you be staying for the service?'

"Yes sir, I will be."

Jason took his seat towards the back of the temple. He could see Cassidy towards the front. She turned and saw him taking his seat and looked surprised that he was sitting in on the service. Five minutes into the service, Jason regretted attending. He spent the first thirty minutes of silent reflection wondering if he could sneak out unnoticed. It was the same stupid, meaningless stuff that it had always been. During the second portion, when temple-goers raised concerns, Jason decided he'd had enough. He got up and tried to squeeze his way out of the pew saying "excuse me" to try to get past annoyed-looking lizards on his way towards the exit. He tried to open the door as quietly as possible, but given how old the building was, there was a loud screeching sound. Most people in the temple turned to see what it was, including Cassidy. They made eye contact for a split second. Jason could see the disappointment in her face. He made an apologetic gesture for disrupting the service and turned and left. At least he left before people started licking that damned disease-infested cup.

Chapter 52

Mr. Ruggles had a busy morning that, unfortunately, he had little to show for. He swung by Buff's to talk with Gary Dupler about getting back in business together. Gary had added more exercise equipment since the last time Mr. Ruggles had visited. There were at least three or four new machines that looked like they were designed to let lizard's run in place. There were so many beautiful trails around Scalestown. You could run through the woods on the soft dirt. You could run by the water with a cool breeze washing over you. Mr. Ruggles had no idea why someone would want to run without actually going anywhere.

Gary was hesitant about reviving their business relationship and said to come back after sales at the store had picked up. He got the same answer from the nursing home, although they were not as direct as Gary was with their answer. After dancing around the issue to avoid feelings getting hurt, Mr. Ruggles realized it was a lost cause, thanked them for their time, and left. He called Hal Poland from the school committee who laughed him off the phone and barely gave him the time of day. Mr. Ruggles tried to remain positive. His spirits skyrocketed when he got back to Donuts on Blanch and saw lizards hanging around outside trying to see if they were open. He then spoke with Jason. Jason filled him in on his experiences in front of the diner, behind the school yard, and at Temple and predicted a full house tomorrow morning.

Jason was indeed correct. The next morning, the line was around the corner just like it used to be.

Chapter 53

Six months passed by. Quality of life in Scalestown as a whole was decreasing somewhat dramatically. Unemployment rates were at an all-time high, businesses were closing, and non-violent crime rates involving things like breaking and entering were on a record-breaking upward trajectory. Furthermore, school attendance rates were down as was attendance at Temple. Even at Scalestown's lowest points, the Temple had remained busy and had helped hold the community together through the tough times. Downtown Scalestown was starting to resemble the way it had looked years prior to the revitalization project that Mr. Ruggles had helped spearhead. It seemed as though the rich were getting richer, as the average Scalestown resident saw their quality of life plummeting. The local government was scrambling to try to turn things around but was unable to identify the root cause of the issues. Based on projections, homelessness could start becoming a real issue in the town as well. A lot of students couldn't afford school lunch. Many felt the government should cover this cost. Many thought the government should cover costs around public housing as well as increase taxes on successful businesses. Some were going as far as saying the government should pay residents a wage just for being a resident. Where was that money going to come from though? With less business came less tax revenue for the town. With less business came fewer jobs and more lizards falling out of higher tax brackets. Lizards wanted to find a solution, but there was no easy solution that could be agreed upon. The few successful businesses that remained were feeling pressure from the community to do their part to help out. There was a new wave of lizards running for City Council promising radical change. This had current City Counselors, and successful business owners, nervous and was creating a bigger divide in the community.

But Mr. Ruggles was doing well. He was making more money from Donuts on Blanch than he ever had with any of his past business ventures. Despite the economic downturn, lizards were scrounging up what little money they could to spend on the delicious treats that provided a brief distraction from their problems. While the number of clients at his dry cleaners had dropped, it didn't matter. Mr. Ruggles' biggest concern now was the possibility of leadership changes that could impact his bank account. When he had helped lead the charge to revitalize downtown Scalestown years ago, he worked diligently to roll back taxes on businesses to encourage new ones to open and existing ones to stay within city limits. This was now in danger of being undone.

Chapter 54

Dustin too was doing well. At least financially. While the number of businesses he could collect payments from was decreasing due to the growing number going out of business, he was making more money than Vladdy could count from the Haverfords deal. Vladdy was spending most of his time now building political connections and doing what he could to protect their business interests. They were focusing more on creating legitimate revenue streams. But a potential change on City Council could lead to the appointment of a new Police Commissioner—perhaps one that would not be as sympathetic to their cause. Vladdy thought it best to cover their tracks to be able to present themselves as legitimate to hide the illegal money coming through. They also wanted to keep their involvement in the Haverfords deal quiet. Some of their money was being sent over to Beverly Lowery to continue to publish articles about how Haverfords was providing jobs to the community and, without it, the town would be certain to see the downward trends spiral out of control even further. It got to the point where Pauric was getting bored at his lack of utilization. He still collected from a handful of businesses on a weekly basis, but the traditional tactics around intimidation and violence were not as prevalent as they had been in the past. They did not want to draw any negative attention to themselves when the town was on the decline. Dustin actually had to increase Pauric's pay to keep him from taking out his aggression and frustrations on local patrons at Wild Wilma's.

Dustin was conflicted, however. He was part of the Scalestown community and seeing the rapid decline pained him. Was he a criminal profiting from the entire situation? Absolutely. But seeing young lizards missing out on a solid education or parents not being able to provide for their families and being forced to live in the streets was difficult to watch. While Dustin was ruthless when it came to dealing with other shady lizards partaking in illicit activities, he had a soft spot for Scalestown as a whole. Vladdy was the more ruthless one when it came to profiting off of the every-day lizard. He hadn't grown up here, Dustin had to remind himself. Dustin started looking into organizations he could make anonymous donations to that could help the every-day-lizard of Scalestown. He wanted to make sure it went towards a good cause and was handled by someone competent.

Chapter 55

Jason's wallet remained fat. He had gotten several raises as the success of Donuts on Blanch continued. Despite his financial growth, he found himself caring less and less about his work. He was questioning what he wanted to do with his life. As the days passed, he was growing more convinced that it was not to serve donuts all day long. He considered going back to school but didn't have the energy while working full-time. He had started making excuses to skip work just to lay around and watch TV. Mr. Ruggles was probably getting suspicious with his increasing absences but had not said anything so far. Would Jason care if he got fired? Maybe. But maybe not. He had gotten his own apartment, so he was no longer stuck on Oliver's couch like a child. Although, his diet still consisted mainly of donuts and macaroni. He had not found another lady lizard to fill the void of loneliness that existed since the post-Cassidy era.

The community was struggling, Jason knew. Both statistically and by virtue of his own observations. The town looked sadder as a whole. The bright smiling faces that used to stand in line at Donuts on Blanch had been replaced with hollow stares. A lot of the lizards waiting in line looked like they could use a shower or a fresh outfit. Stop coming here every day, Jason thought to himself. Save up this money and buy some decent clothes. Why wouldn't they do that? It's almost like they needed it. Then he'd take a bite of a donut and could empathize that the brief moment of joy may outweigh the benefits of a fresh shirt.

Plenty of lizards were getting frustrated and were trying to do something about it. Jason just didn't care enough to take any sort of action. At times, he wasn't sure if he even wanted to keep living. Based on articles he read in the *Lizard Daily*, Jason knew he was not alone with these feelings. According to a recent article, the suicide rate in Scalestown was on the rise. Jason wasn't seriously considering it. Yet, anyways. So, he continued his mundane routine feeling less motivated and more lethargic with each passing day.

Chapter 56

Dustin had also seen the article about the rising rate of suicides in Scalestown. It was a sensitive subject for him, although he tried to block it out. Over the past few years, Dustin had started to question whether his mother's death was the result of an accidental fire, or if it was one she had started on purpose to escape this world. It wasn't until he read an article about depression published by Dr. Arthur Verner (the same doctor that authored the study on the benefits of exercise) two years back that he started questioning what had happened. From a distance, Dustin's mother, Darlene, appeared like a happy-go-lucky, optimistic go-getter. When reading the article on depression, some of the characteristics covered sounded familiar. His mother's long stretches without sleep, unpredictable mood swings, and lack of appetite all checked the boxes.

At first, he thought maybe his father leaving them had caused the depression to kick in. Dustin had hated him for it. After more reflection, however, Dustin started remembering instances when he was younger, when his father was still around, that were disturbing. There was a time when he was very young where he remembered waking up in the middle of the night hearing a whimpering sound accompanied by a light knocking of a door. Dustin crawled out of bed and pried his door open slightly. His father was seated at the bathroom door speaking softly, almost as if confiding secrets to it. If the door was listening, it wasn't replying. Was his dad sleep walking? Why was he talking to a door? Dustin remembered hearing a muffled cry of pain come from the bathroom. His dad started frantically whispering his mother's name while turning the door handle back and forth. After confirming the door was still locked, Dustin's father kicked it with all his might. Dustin jumped in surprise. His father saw Dustin and told him to go back to bed. He tried to sound calm, but, even at a young age, Dustin could tell he was far from calm. His father turned and kicked the door a second time. And then a third. Finally, the door collapsed. Dustin's father rushed in and let out an anguished groan. Although he was scared, Dustin peered into the bathroom and saw his mother lying on the floor next to a pool of red liquid. Blood, Dustin knew. He had seen it come out of his friend's nose after a soccer ball hit him in the face one day at recess.

His mother looked up and saw Dustin standing there. She did her best to muster up a smile and said, "Mommy accidently cut herself on the shower faucet. Tobias, go get Dustin back into bed." Dustin had never noticed the shower faucet being sharp, but now he would be sure to proceed with extra caution when he was in the tub.

After recalling this incident, Dustin then started wondering if his father, Tobias, had left because he couldn't handle her depression. If his mother did start the fire on purpose, why did she give up on Dustin and leave him all alone? Was he not worth living for? This re-directed Dustin's anger towards her. Talk about selfish. What if it had been his fault though? He hadn't provided enough support or joy in her life to keep her from doing such a thing? He hated himself.

Dustin eventually came to terms that he didn't know all the facts and that it wasn't productive or healthy to harbor anger towards anyone when he didn't know for sure what had happened. Accepting that allowed him to drop some of that baggage he was carrying and move on but reading that suicide rates were on the rise in Scalestown was a painful walk down memory lane. He decided he needed to start doing more for his community. That night, Dustin Tisburry, the most dangerous lizard in Scalestown, sat down at his kitchen table and started mapping out where he could start donating money. He went to bed smiling for the first time in a long time.

Chapter 57

Mr. Ruggles had been hounding Casper Fitzpatrick's office all week trying to get in touch with the City Councilor. He had a good, mutually beneficial relationship with Casper. They had both helped with the Scalestown Downtown Revitalization project and Casper was pro-business, which meant that Mr. Ruggles was pro-Casper. He had helped support Casper, vocally and financially, on his rise to City Council. Casper was on the hot seat as election-time was a mere eight weeks away. The deterioration of Scalestown on his watch did not reflect well, especially since his calling card had always been the strength of the local economy. There was, however, a new voice in Scalestown politics. One of hope, reform, and change by the common lizard, for the common lizard. One that was passionate and genuine. The voice belonged to Kerry Bolkanski.

Kerry had popped onto the political spectrum out of nowhere. She was a schoolteacher who served as a liaison with the school committee but had no political experience at any level. Kerry had a couple of young kids and was campaigning against the gloomy prospect of growing up in a place like Scalestown should the downward trajectory continue to spiral out of control. Their family picture was plastered on fliers all over Scalestown with slogans about new faces, bold ideas, and positive changes. Mr. Ruggles had met her when he went to the School Committee meeting to talk about incorporating donuts into the school's cafeterias. They had exchanged a brief hello upon introduction, but Mr. Ruggles barely remembered the interaction. She was smart. Smarter than Casper; no doubt about it.

Mr. Ruggles was finally able to get in touch with Casper. They jumped right past the chit-chat and started talking about the campaign. They agreed that if Scalestown weren't in such a rough patch, her campaign would have been a joke. But Casper Fitzpatrick was not laughing. And neither was Mr. Ruggles.

Chapter 58

Jason started running out of excuses for missing work. He knew he should feel badly since Mr. Ruggles had been more than generous to him. At first, it didn't seem like the absences were an issue. After all, shit happens. But Jason started to sense that Mr. Ruggles had not only grown suspicious, but also tired of his behavior. One morning, Jason was a half an hour late to a shift. Mr. Ruggles pulled him aside to the back office and asked him if he still wanted the job. Jason reassured him it wouldn't happen again. The next morning, Jason was late. Mr. Ruggles signaled him to the back room.

Jason had never noticed that they were the same height. Mr. Ruggles wore a checkered ascot tie, mocha-brown leather shoes, and a bowler hat—successfully pulling off the sophisticated look he was always going for.

"Jason," Mr. Ruggles began, "I don't know what's been going on with you. I must say I'm very disappointed. It's unfortunate that it's come to this. You're fired."

Jason looked back at him knowing he should feel embarrassed or disappointed or upset or guilty, but he didn't feel any of those things—he just wanted the conversation to end so he could hang up his apron and never take another donut order for the rest of his life.

"I understand. I appreciate the opportunity and am sorry I let you down, sir," Jason replied.

Mr. Ruggles looked at him curiously, then shook his head. He reached into his back pocket to take out his wallet, "Here's your last paycheck. Good luck in the future, Jason."

With that, Mr. Ruggles turned and left the kitchen. Jason debated poking his head into the kitchen and saying goodbye to Mathieu. Although he was quiet, he was a good guy and Jason had grown to enjoy his company. Instead of bidding Mathieu farewell, he removed his apron, threw it in the trash, grabbed 5 boxes of packaged donuts off the counter, and headed out the back door.

Things got worse from there. He fell behind on his rental payments. He had no money for groceries. Each morning, Jason would walk over to Donuts on Blanch. He was too embarrassed to go inside so would tap on the back door. Mathieu would come out and give him a couple of donuts. He'd then walk to the park and sit and eat his donuts and stare out over the water. At no time did he consider looking for a new job. Two weeks later, he got the eviction notice from his landlord. He called Oliver, despite their falling out, to see if he could book a reservation on the living room couch. When they spoke, Oliver was friendly enough but told Jason that he had moved out of Scalestown several weeks ago after accepting a new job offer elsewhere. Jason thought he could always fall back on Oliver's. Now that it was no longer an option, the reality and gravity of the situation started to kick in. He had very little money, no job, and no place to stay. He considered calling Cassidy and begging her to take him back but decided against it. There was now a sizable homeless community that lived by the bridge over near the park where Jason would eat his donuts each morning. So, Jason Alfonso, a lizard in the prime years of his life who, until recently, had a steady paycheck and a nice apartment, packed up what belongings he could carry and wandered over to the bridge to set up a makeshift shelter he could call home.

There were even more lizards down by the bridge than Jason had realized. From the park, you could only see a fraction of the population. It was like its own little town. Jason began walking up and down the rows of homemade tents. There were plenty of lizards who looked much worse off than he did. Some sat in their tents looking out aimlessly. Others were gathered in groups playing card games or telling stories of happier times. Jason saw an area that appeared open that was under a tree. Perhaps enough cover to stay dry when it rains and to keep the sun off his back when it gets hot. He walked over and started unpacking his things when he heard a grunt.

"What the hell do you think you're doing kid?" It was one of the rude lizards who had given him a hard time at the donut shop after they stopped serving the original recipe. If the lizard recognized Jason, he did not show it. It felt like a lifetime ago.

"Sorry, this spot looked open, so I was going to lay down here," Jason said. He looked around to see if there was some doctrine outlining the rules and regulations of this section of town. From what he could tell it was jungle-law.

"Well, it isn't open. So, get your shit out of here," the lizard snapped back.

Jason gathered his things. Someone else called over to him.

"Hey man, come over here a minute." The voice sounded younger and much friendlier. Jason looked up and saw a lizard waving him over. He was probably ten years older than Jason.

Jason waved back and headed across the path to meet him.

"I'm Artie. I've been living over here about two months. Here, there's some open space on the other side of my tent. Ignore that guy, he's a dick to everyone. I'll show you the ropes."

"Thanks," Jason replied.

He walked around to the other side of Artie's tent. There wasn't much room, but at least there were no signs of sharp rocks. It would have to do.

Chapter 59

Dustin got word that an alarming number of children could not afford school lunch. The school had tried giving it out for free, but it wasn't sustainable financially. Dustin thought back to when he was in school. The lunches weren't anything to write home about. It was an average portion of average, at best, food in a menu that rotated very infrequently. Still, the thought of not having a lunch and sitting through the whole day hungry sounded much worse. Dustin decided this would be a good first step at giving back to Scalestown. But how? He didn't want anyone to know it was him. That would bring questions about where his money came from—how he had so much of it, why it was never taxed, etc. Dustin chuckled to himself. After all he had done, he was struggling to figure out how to donate money to a school. Dustin did some digging and discovered that Hal Poland was on the PTA. Hal had been in Dustin's graduating class back when they were at Scalestown High. He wasn't someone Dustin had spoken to, or thought of, in many years. They had always gotten along. Dustin wasn't sure if Hal knew about his, shall we say, career progression since high school. The tone of Hal's voice at the beginning of their phone conversation suggested that he was, in fact, aware of Dustin's post-graduation accomplishments.

"Hello?" Dustin recognized Hal's voice, even after all these years.

"Hi, is this Hal?"

"It is, yes. May I ask who's calling?" Hal replied.

"Yes, Hal, this is Dustin Tisburry. Long-time, no talk," Dustin said.

There was an awkward pause. Hal was most likely wracking his brain trying to think what he had possibly done to warrant this call. He also may have been wondering if he should address him as Dustin or Daddy Long Tongue.

"Hey Dustin—wow, it's been a while. What can I do for you?" Hal replied, anxiously.

"I've heard that students are having a tough time paying for school lunches and that there isn't much the school can do to help. I'd like to help but I wasn't sure how to go about doing so. I found out you're on the PTA, and, since we go back a way, figured I'd reach out," Dustin said.

"Wow, ok. That's great to hear. What'd you have in mind?" Hal asked. He still sounded nervous and a little confused.

"I'd like to fund free lunches for every student for the rest of the school year."

"Wow. Ok. Um...wow," Hal stammered.

Since he didn't ask anything about where the money would be coming from or give a warning about how expensive it would be, Dustin figured it was safe to assume that Hal was familiar with his lifestyle.

"I want the donation to be anonymous. For obvious reasons, I don't want any inquiries about where the money came from or how it was made," Dustin said.

Another long pause. "This is an incredibly generous offer. Just to make sure we're on the same page...you are aware there is no way the school could pay this debt back with or without interest anytime in the near future, correct?" Hal asked. Dustin could tell he was worried he was walking on thin ice.

"Hal, the money comes with no strings attached. I want to help these kids and this community. All I want is discretion on your end about where the money came from. At the beginning of each month, give me an estimate of what you think lunch costs will come out to, and I'll pay you up front. I can have an associate drop it off where and when it is convenient for you. And Hal, just to be perfectly clear, this money goes to the kids. If I find out that it ends up in other people's hands, I'll be quite upset."

Hal replied quickly this time, "Of course. Of course. Well, this is fantastic news and will go a long way to make positive changes in the school. Thank you very much, Dustin. I mean it."

Chapter 6U

The election was now two weeks away. Kerry Bolkanski was surging in the polls. She was a mere two points behind Casper. Mr. Ruggles decided to do something he never had done before—call Vladdy directly. He figured that Vladdy wanted Casper to win as badly as he did. Kerry's first focus could very well be Haverfords as it represented the out-of-town conglomerate that she had been targeting in a lot of her messaging. Mr. Ruggles knew Dustin wouldn't be involved at this level. Vladdy was surprisingly receptive to his call and they agreed to meet for lunch.

"Good afternoon Mr. Ruggles. I must admit, I was a little caught off guard by your call," Vladdy said as he extended his hand.

"Hello, Vladdy. Yes, my assumption was that our interests in Casper retaining his seat on City Council were closely aligned," Mr. Ruggles replied.

Vladdy nodded in agreement. "Yes, they certainly are. We've been trying to dig up some dirt on her but can't seem to find any. So, I've decided we're going to create our own dirt. I was speaking with Beverly Lowery at the paper last evening about running a story about a scandalous extramarital affair Kerry had with a fellow teacher."

Mr. Ruggles couldn't help but wince at Beverly's name. She had caused him a lot of issues in the past. "So, this affair is fabricated then?"

"Yes. We'll have Beverly quote an anonymous source or two and hope that it does some damage with people who just read the headline," Vladdy said without a hint of sympathy for trying to sabotage this woman's life. He continued, "What if you come out afterwards and, in light of this news, publicly endorse Casper?"

Mr. Ruggles thought it over. "If she wins, this would make me an easy target with the proposed tax increases."

"If she wins, your taxes are going up regardless of what you say now," Vladdy argued.

It was a fair point. "Ok, I'll do it. But I won't talk to Beverly. Someone else will need to write that article." Mr. Ruggles was not going to give her the satisfaction.

Vladdy nodded in understanding.

"Does Casper know?" Mr. Ruggles asked.

"No, he doesn't. But if he wins, we'll let him know who helped pave the way to his victory," Vladdy said with a smirk.

"When will it go to print?" Mr. Ruggles asked.

"I'll speak with her this afternoon and see if she can get it to print tomorrow. You can then weigh in with your thoughts and endorsement to make the paper the following day," Vladdy said.

The two lizards shook hands, paid the bill, and went their separate ways.

Sure enough, the paper the following morning dropped the bombshell news to Scalestown.

Inappropriate behavior from City Council hopeful Kerry Bolkanski?

By Beverly Lowery

Kerry Bolkanski's popularity as a potential new City Council member has skyrocketed over the past several weeks. She's running on a platform of reform—to help the everyday Scalestown resident return to a better quality of life. Part of what makes her an extremely popular candidate is her character. She's a schoolteacher who has done a lot of good for the community and stands for family values. That's why the rumors currently circulating around a potential extramarital affair could be very damaging to her campaign. I've spoken to two sources, who wish to stay anonymous, that Kerry was having an affair with a fellow teacher at Scalestown High. I reached out to Kerry's campaign for comment and have yet to hear back. Current City Councilman Casper Fitzpatrick said of the incident, "It's extremely disappointing to hear this news about Kerry Bolkanski. For someone who claims to have strong moral fiber, this certainly shows a different side of things." With the election approaching rapidly, we'll see how this impacts Bolkanski's campaign.

The following morning, the article with Mr. Ruggles' comments was published.

Prominent businessman weighs in on City Council scandal; endorses Casper Fitzpatrick

By Amir Kalil

Mr. Ruggles, the owner of several successful businesses in Scalestown including the wildly popular Donuts on Blanch was asked to comment on the breaking news yesterday around a potential affair that Kerry Bolkanski had with a fellow teacher. Mr. Ruggles said, "I usually try to stay out of politics. I work hard and run my business and trust the people of Scalestown to elect the leaders they believe in most. We're at a trying time in Scalestown right now, though. I don't think it's a wise idea to elect someone to a position of power who acts unethically. I am, therefore, endorsing Casper Fitzpatrick in his race for City Council."

Over the next two days, Mr. Ruggles watched as Casper's lead over Kerry jumped a few points. It looked like Vladdy's strategy was paying off.

Chapter 61

Kerry Bolkanski sat on her couch. She was both terrified and excited. It was election night, and the final results were being tallied. Heading into the night, she was the underdog. Initial reporting was showing that the voting was just about a 50/50 split. It was anyone's game.

She was seated next to her husband, Richard. He went by Richie. Richie was a town official responsible for overseeing the sanitation department. There were plenty of jokes over the years about how Richie had a "shitty" job...none of which were particularly funny. They had put their kids to bed an hour ago as the election was dragging on later into the evening than was anticipated.

Richie was hesitant about Kerry running for office. He was worried about her being put in a position to fail. Her passion and resolve changed his mind and he, rather quickly, supported the campaign.

Even with the long campaigning hours, plus continued work at the school, their relationship had held up just fine. That is, until Beverly Lowery published her article about the alleged affair. At first, Richie was beyond hurt. It took Kerry several days to convince Richie that it was political sabotage directed at her because she was making the opposition nervous with her mission to change the status-quo. When no other evidence was uncovered, Richie believed her and supported her even more in her mission.

Beverly Lowery, that bitch, Kerry thought to herself. Kerry and Beverly had gone to school with each other and had gotten along quite well. While they had

fallen out of touch over the years, Kerry was shocked, and disappointed when she
saw it was Beverly who had written the article about the alleged affair.

Lost in her thoughts, Kerry was brought back to the present by a firm, supportive squeeze of her hand by Richie. They were about to make the final announcement. The television flashed her vote number first as the news anchor provided some commentary. Kerry tried to do some quick mental math in her head to see if it was more than half of the Scalestown population, but her mind was too distracted. She could never have imagined earning this number of votes when she started her campaign. The winner's vote tally would surely be shown second, not first, to increase the dramatic effect, right? Casper's final vote tally flashed across the screen—it was six votes lower than Kerry's. Richie wrapped her up in a big hug and shouted in victory. Kerry hugged him back and let out a victory yell of her own. The children came rushing down the stairs trying to discern if these were shouts of joy or pain. They quickly joined the celebration of their mother's triumph.

The phone rang—it was Casper calling to congratulate her on the win. As is custom, he offered to meet her at City Hall in the morning to bring her up to speed on the current status of several important issues as well as to give her the keys to his office. He told her he was truly impressed with her campaign and offered to be supportive in the transition period. Casper also denied any involvement with the fabricated story that was published about her "affair" and said he hoped she believed him. He sounded sincere, but Kerry wasn't convinced. Regardless, it was in the past.

The phone rang a second time. This time a voice greeted her on the other end that she did not recognize.

"Mrs. Bolkanski?" the voice asked. "Or should I say councilwoman Bolkanski."

"Yes, this is she," Kerry replied. Councilwoman Bolkanski had a nice ring to it.

"I've been rooting for you to win," the voice said.

"Well, I appreciate the support," Kerry said.

"I was too nervous to bring this to anyone's attention but, now that you've won your seat on City Council, I feel like I have an obligation to," the voice sounded gravely serious.

Kerry realized she was having trouble hearing the person on the other end of the phone over the Bol-Kan-Ski chants Richie was leading their kids in. She put her hand over the phone and waved at Richie to get his attention. She smiled and mouthed at him to take the kids upstairs to bed. He must have seen the serious look in her eyes because he escorted them upstairs without inquiring about who was on the other end of the line. The room was now silent.

"What is it you'd like to tell me?" Kerry asked, trying to sound confident.

"I know what's been wreaking havoc on Scalestown," the voice said with a pause. Kerry paused as well to see if the voice would continue. "It's Haverfords."

Kerry's heart skipped a beat. "How so?"

"There's been some sort of poison that's been leaking into the water supply. This is what has been causing everyone to be acting so crazy."

"How do you know this?" Kerry asked, desperately.

"I used to work there until very recently." Kerry detected fear in this lizard's voice. "You'll look into it, won't you?"

"Of course, I will," Kerry said. "Do you have any other information? Any proof?"

"No, unfortunately not. But if you have someone dig into it, I think you'll find it pretty easily."

Chapter 62

Word of the election results had not reached Jason or Bridgetown— what the locals now called the community living under the bridge. It didn't seem like anyone had been following it, even though this population likely had the most to gain from Kerry Bolkanski's victory. Jason hadn't exercised his right to vote this time around. Instead, Jason and Artie were playing cards in his tent. It had rained the night before, leaving the ground damp and cold. Water was seeping through the bottom of the tent into Jason's pants. The mud was caked under his toenails and between the scales on his tail. He desperately needed a shower.

Jason and Artie had developed quite a friendship. He discovered he could open up to Artie in a more honest and truthful way than he was able to with Oliver or even Cassidy. Perhaps it was because they were both going through the same struggles and had similar questions about life's purpose. Jason was appreciative that Artie was showing him the ropes in his new community and Artie was appreciative that Jason brought back free donuts. Jason still went knocking each morning on the back door of Donuts on Blanch, and Mathieu, without fail, continued to give him a box of free donuts. Jason and Artie quickly discovered they needed to keep that a secret from their neighbors or else there would be an all-out battle for the donuts, down to the last crumb. From time to time, Jason could use the donuts as a form of currency to trade for a fresh pair of socks, bottle of soda, pack of cards, or various other items essential to survival down by

Bridgetown. Bridgetown had no formal government, just an unspoken constitution providing basic guidelines for how lizards should behave. Jason may officially be a resident of Scalestown, but Bridgetown was now his home.

Chapter 63

Mr. Ruggles and Vladdy met the following day for breakfast. The mood was subdued after the election results from the night before. Neither lizard spoke for several minutes.

"I still can't believe it," Mr. Ruggles said.

"Neither can I," Vladdy replied.

"Have you spoken to Casper at all?" Mr. Ruggles asked.

"Yes, earlier this morning. Kerry will be in his office towards the end of the day to get briefed," Vladdy said.

Mr. Ruggles leaned in closer and whispered, "What about any sensitive information Casper might have on his computer or in his office?" Two checks that Mr. Ruggles had written to Casper's campaign that exceeded the legal donation amount came to mind. There were also a few quid-pro-quo emails that surely breached ethical barriers, if not legal ones.

"Pauric and I are headed over there right after this. Pauric will search the office and ensure anything that we may not want to be discovered is burned. I'll check the computer records and make sure those are permanently deleted. Casper wants them destroyed as well, so it should be a smooth enough process," Vladdy replied. It was clear Vladdy had some dirty laundry over there as well.

"Will you double check on one or two things for me? To make sure they are part of the destruction process?" Mr. Ruggles asked.

"Yes, we can do that," Vladdy said.

Mr. Ruggles scribbled a couple of things down on a napkin and slid it across the table to Vladdy. While he didn't fully trust Vladdy, there was no reason to believe Vladdy wouldn't follow through.

"I'm thinking it might be a good idea if I call Bolkanski and congratulate her on her victory and apologize about my quotes," Mr. Ruggles said.

"It may not be a bad idea to do some sort of good for the community as a show of good faith. A donation to a cause, perhaps," Vladdy said.

"That's a good idea. I'll do that. I read they were struggling with free lunches. Perhaps I can provide free donuts," Mr. Ruggles said.

"Daddy Long Tongue has actually already volunteered to cover all lunch costs," Vladdy said, sounding both amused and disgruntled.

Mr. Ruggles looked back in surprise. "Really? That's interesting. What does he have to gain by doing that?"

"Nothing to gain," Vladdy said while raising his hands up in a shrug. "He's doing it anonymously to help out Scalestown."

"That's quite noble," Mr. Ruggles said. He left out that it sounded odd.

"Yes, quite noble," Vladdy replied, with a hint of sarcasm.

After breakfast, Vladdy headed down towards City Hall. Mr. Ruggles took out his phone and called Councilwoman Bolkanski.

"Hello?" said Kerry Bolkanski's voice. It was quite friendly.

"Hi Councilwoman Bolkanski. This is Mr. Ruggles calling. I was wondering if you had a minute to speak?"

The friendly tone from Kerry's voice hardened. "Oh, hello Mr. Ruggles. Sure, I can talk for a minute."

"First off, congrats on your big win. It was very impressive. Very impressive indeed."

Thank you, Mr. Ruggles. You know, I happened to catch your quotes in the *Lizard Daily* before the election about the false rumors regarding an affair. I'm sure you remember which article I'm talking about?" Kerry said with an obvious hint of sarcasm.

"Well yes, Kerry, I suppose I do. That's part of why I wanted to call. I should have phrased that quote better and said, 'if it is true' before sharing my opinion. If it were true, I would stand by the statement and stand by my quote. I shouldn't have believed what I read in the press without speaking to you about it first. Meelosh only knows that Beverly Lowery has slandered my name in print before. So, for that I apologize," Mr. Ruggles said.

"I appreciate that, Mr. Ruggles. Is there anything else I can do for you?" she asked.

Mr. Ruggles was thrown off a bit by her brashness. She hadn't even officially been in office yet and was giving him this attitude? He started getting angry himself but gulped it back down to the pit of his stomach. "I think it's important for hard working local business owners to build relationships with local government to make sure our community is thriving in the best possible way."

"Thriving like it is now?" Kerry asked.

"Could there be a more important time to pull together and align than now?" Mr. Ruggles flipped back around on her. "I had a meeting scheduled with Casper for later this week about giving back to the community especially given the circumstances. I'd like to have that conversation with you. Is that something that could be arranged?"

"Yes," Kerry replied. "Once I get settled in, I will reach out and we can set something up."

Ben Stephenson

Mr. Ruggles wasn't expecting her to be quite as firm as she was. Was firm the right word? Aggressive—no, not aggressive. Regardless, she caught him off guard. Maybe it wouldn't be quite as easy to win her good graces as he initially thought.

Chapter 64

Dustin was expecting Beverly Lowery any minute. She had called him last night saying she needed to meet. There was a sense of urgency in her voice that he hadn't heard before. She suggested meeting somewhere in town, but Dustin did not want to be seen out in the public with a well-known member of the press.

Dustin had known Beverly for a long time. He was friends with her older brother, Damian, when they were growing up. There was a pretty big age gap between them and Beverly, but he knew her, nonetheless. Damian had passed away several years ago after being sick for a long time. Dustin visited him in the hospital and could barely recognize his old friend. When he heard Damian had passed, he felt relieved. The Damian he knew would not have wanted to continue living in the condition he had been.

Beverly was heart-broken at the funeral and could hardly control her emotions. She had just started at the paper earlier that year and was making entry-level newspaper pay—which isn't much. Dustin offered to pay for the funeral service. At first, she declined the offer but after seeing how expensive it would all be, swallowed her pride and reached back out to say she would take him up on it after all. After the funeral they got to talking, and Dustin asked if she would like to make more money. He'd keep her on his payroll, and all she had to do was tweak an article here or there. Sometimes it was to dismiss something that could be seen as negative, sometimes it was to discredit his enemies, other times, like with the

Haverfords deal, it was justification of his behind-the-scenes decision making. While he didn't have to lean on her as a resource too frequently, it had been a wise investment. It was mutually beneficial. Beverly made money on the side, and some of the information she got from Dustin and Vladdy helped launch her career to become the top journalist in town.

Beverly arrived. She entered the house and greeted Dustin. Dustin offered her a cup of tea, which she accepted. He motioned for her to take a seat on the couch while he went into the kitchen to remove the hissing tea kettle from the burner. He pulled out two mugs from his cabinet and dropped teabags into them. He returned the kettle to the stovetop and headed back into the living room to deliver her cup of tea. She thanked him but did not give the cup a second glance.

"What's up, Beverly?" he asked. She did not look like she was in the mood for small talk.

"Thanks for seeing me on such short notice." She paused as if trying to gather her thoughts. "I received a phone call last night from Kerry Bolkanski."

"Ah, our new Councilwoman?" Dustin asked.

"Correct. She said she got an anonymous phone call the night of the election—after the results were finalized and it was announced that she was the winner. The caller claims that Haverfords is poisoning the water supply. Poisoning may not be the right word. The caller wasn't sure if it was intentional or if it was a byproduct of the operation. According to the caller, this is what is leading to the strange and irrational behavior that has caused an increase in crime and homelessness and the decline in quality of life, attendance rate for schools and the overall lack or caring in the community."

There was a long pause. Dustin tried to absorb the information.

Beverly continued, "Kerry asked if he had any sort of proof. He said he unfortunately did not but that if someone dug around it could be uncovered quickly. It does seem like the timelines fit in — the town started to deteriorate after Haverfords arrival."

Still, Dustin sat silently.

Beverly looked uncomfortable with the silence and jumped back in to avoid it, "Anyways, I figured I would alert you first and see what you wanted me to do."

"Thank you, Beverly. Why did Kerry come to you with this?" Dustin asked.

"We went to school together and ran track and field. She called and we talked about the article I had written about her affair. She was upset about that. I apologized and explained I was just doing my job. We've known each other for a long time though, so she trusts me, I guess. She filled me in on the phone call and asked if I'd look into it. She said she didn't want to go to the police with no evidence when she just started the position. I think she's hoping I can dig up enough that she can put something a little more formal in place before going public. A big part of her platform when she was campaigning was around the negative impact of out-of-town big business. This could be a big win for her politically. I think she cares about the town as well—not your run-of-the-mill politician like Casper Fitzpatrick."

"How did you leave things with her?" Dustin asked.

Beverly replied, "I told her I would look into it and get back to her."

"Good. Thanks for bringing this to me. It's the first I'm hearing of it, so I don't have an answer on the best way to move forward with it yet. Can you stall her?"

"Of course. When should I expect to hear from you by?" Beverly asked.

"I don't know. But I will be in touch," Dustin said, trying to keep his voice steady.

He thanked her again and walked her to the door. She hadn't touched her tea. It was still hot since their conversation had been quick and to the point. He scooped up Beverly's cup and started sipping on it. Could this be true? Was

Haverfords causing this whole mess? Were the bastards doing it on purpose or was it an unknown error? Dustin's blood started to boil at the thought of them doing it on purpose—not only for damaging the community but also trying to pull one over on him. He took a couple of deep breaths and continued to sip the tea. He was probably jumping to conclusions. There was no evidence besides one nut-job making a phone call. Vladdy was supposed to be coming over within the hour. Dustin took his phone out and texted him saying he wasn't feeling well and wanted to reschedule for tomorrow. He needed to think.

Chapter 65

Mr. Ruggles received a text message. He barely ever got text messages. Hell, he wasn't sure if he even knew how to reply to one. It was tough to hit those small buttons accurately with his scaly fingers. This one was from Dustin. It was asking him to come over that evening. There were no other details provided. He replied to Dustin, happy that the phone auto-corrected his typing errors, saying he could be there at 8pm.

Mr. Ruggles arrived at Dustin's residence at 8pm. Dustin greeted him and ushered him into the living room. He offered him a seat on the couch and asked if he wanted a glass of scotch. Mr. Ruggles was surprised—when was the last time Dustin had casually invited him for a drink? He could use a good glass of scotch, so, per usual when it was offered, Mr. Ruggles accepted.

"I need your advice on something, Mr. Ruggles," Dustin began. Mr. Ruggles must have looked pleasantly surprised because Dustin smiled and continued, "I know it's been a while since I've asked that."

"Of course, Dustin. You haven't needed much over the recent years, but I'd like to think I gave you some decent advice when you were a younger lizard," Mr. Ruggles said.

Dustin gave a quick acknowledging nod of the head. "It came to my attention today that Haverfords may be causing some of the awful trends and behaviors going on in the community right now. Something about chemicals in the water supply that's been making people act crazy. The person who told me had no proof, so I don't have much to go on. Obviously, Haverfords makes me a lot of money. More money than I've ever made with any of my other ventures. But if it is in fact hurting Scalestown, I don't know if I can continue to do business with them. This could be completely made up; I have no evidence to be sure. Therefore, I certainly don't want to damage that relationship by making accusations left and right. I'm in a bit of a predicament."

Mr. Ruggles smiled gently. He'd be lying to say he wasn't flattered that Dustin was seeking his council. It had been many years since Mr. Ruggles had acted as a father-like figure to him. "It's quite noble that you're considering digging into it instead of just covering it up for the money. Not every lizard could say they would do that. What does Vladdy think?"

"I haven't told him yet. He's not from here. He has no stake in this community. He didn't grow up in Scalestown like we did. My guess is he'd chase the money. Which is why I came to you first," Dustin said.

"That makes sense. I think Scalestown has both been there for us in the past when we've experienced hardships—it's difficult to replicate that feeling for someone who hasn't received that same type of treatment," Mr. Ruggles replied.

Again, Dustin nodded in agreement.

"Well, you want to do the right thing...but you don't want to jeopardize your relationship or lose out on any money if it isn't true. I think that's the right approach. Why not get the water tested and see if there is some sort of chemical or pollution that could be causing the damage? That way, if nothing turns up, you can forget about it. If it does, then you're armed with that information when you go to talk to Douglas Trulio," Mr. Ruggles said.

Dustin took in the information and then started nodding, "That sounds like a good idea to me. How would I go about getting the water supply tested?"

Mr. Ruggles paused, "Great question. I'm not sure I know how."

The two lizards sat in silence drinking their scotch. After a few minutes, Mr. Ruggles said, "Let me sleep on it. I do my best thinking in the morning."

"Fair enough," Dustin said with a slight smile. "Thanks for swinging by, Mr. Ruggles."

Mr. Ruggles got to his car before turning on his heels and reversing his direction back towards Dustin's front door. He knocked. Dustin looked surprised to see him there.

"Did you forget something?" he asked.

"Maybe I just do my best thinking after I finish a nice glass of scotch," Mr. Ruggles said with a grin. "What about going to Dr. Arthur Verner? You know, the doctor who did the study on the health benefits of exercise?"

And the study on depression, Dustin thought to himself. He replied to Mr. Ruggles saying, "I like it. Do you have his phone number to get in touch with him? Could you provide an introduction?"

"I do not, unfortunately. I've never spoken with him." After a brief pause, he continued, "But Gary Dupler must have it. He was able to capitalize off that study to make a lot of money on his gym."

"Can you reach out to Gary for me?" Dustin asked.

"I can give him a call right now," Mr. Ruggles replied.

He got Gary on the first ring and had something set up for Dustin for the following afternoon within a matter of seconds. Mr. Ruggles was pleased he was able to help Dustin.

Chapter 66

Dustin was expecting Vladdy in the morning and Dr. Verner in the afternoon. He wanted to bring Vladdy up to speed about the Haverfords situation before speaking with Dr. Verner. As predicted, Vladdy's reaction wasn't filled with sympathy for Scalestown.

"So, there's no proof?" he asked Dustin.

"Not at this time, no," Dustin replied.

"So, we're going to jeopardize this relationship and crazy amount of money with Haverfords because a new politician whose campaign was built on taking down large-scale corporations claims she got an anonymous phone call that they're doing something evil?" Vladdy pressed on.

When he put it like that, Dustin had to agree it did sound a little silly.

"I don't want to jeopardize anything. That's why we'll have Dr. Verner see if he can do any tests. If nothing is wrong...no harm done."

Vladdy hesitated, "What if there is something wrong?"

Dustin replied firmly, "We'll take it one step at a time."

Vladdy nodded. He knew it wasn't his decision to make.

Dr. Arthur Verner showed up at Dustin's residence several hours later. He had grown up in Scalestown until the age of ten before moving with his family west of the city. Dr. Verner had very much enjoyed his childhood in Scalestown and was sad to leave it behind. After leaving Scalestown, he went on to graduate at the top of his class and decided to attend university to study medicine. Doctors at that time were focused on bumps and bruises. Tell me where you're hurt? Ok, let's put some ice on it or put it in a sling or wrap some bandages around it or rub this ointment on there. While this was all well and good, Dr. Verner wanted to think bigger. How could he use his training to proactively prevent medical issues from starting versus trying to fix things once they were already broken? He ended up finding it difficult to support himself financially trying to play the role of scientist, philosopher and healer. Because he needed to pay his rent, he ended up taking a job at a local family medical practice prescribing ice, slings, bandages and ointments, just like the rest of his peers. While he knew he was helping on a small scale, this job did not allow him to make the wide-spread impact he craved. Several years later, an old professor reached out to Dr. Verner and explained there was a program being paid for with government funds to do health-related research. What a rant his father went on upon learning his son was being paid to read books on the tax-payer's dime. Dr. Verner accepted the job and packed his bags. The new job required him to move even further from home. It was at the Institute for Medical Advancement (IFMA) that Dr. Verner started making a name for himself. While he was best known for his study on the health benefits of exercise, he also contributed to in other studies around topics like depression, sleep deprivation, and vaccinations. While at the IFMA, Dr. Verner met a lady lizard, Chloe, on a night out on the town. Given his knowledge of health, he should have known better, but could not resist...and after a night of too many drinks and too much fun, Dr. Verner had a baby on the way. As he was getting to know his newborn son, he was also still getting to know Chloe. They soon learned they did not have all that much in common. When Dr. Verner's son was young, before he was old enough to form memories, Chloe and Dr. Verner agreed to separate while making a pact that they would both play equal roles in the boy's life. The pact didn't last forever though. Around the time his son was ten, Chloe decided she was done with her current life. She hadn't been ready to settle down and needed to stretch those long thin lizard legs Dr. Verner had been attracted to all those years earlier and roam free. It was shortly after this that Dr. Verner decided to move back to Scalestown to raise his son in a familiar, loving community.

Dustin was excited to meet Dr. Verner. He felt as though he had a special connection given his suspicions of his mother suffering from depression. Despite both living in Scalestown for years, Dustin had never met him. The doctor looked incredibly nervous when he walked into the house—almost like he was doing something illegal by just being there. He probably has never done anything wrong in his life, Dustin thought to himself.

"Dr. Verner, it's an absolute pleasure to meet you. I'm a big fan of your work. Thanks for coming on such short notice," Dustin said warmly while extending his hand. "This is my colleague, Vladdy." Vladdy extended his hand also but did not say anything.

"It's nice to meet you both," Dr. Verner said.

"I have something I need help with. I'd like to start with acknowledging that you've probably heard rumors about the type of lizard I am. Most are true. But I want to reassure you that I do care about this community and have its best interests at heart," Dustin said.

Dr. Verner nodded back enthusiastically. It was difficult to tell if he believed him or was just trying to play the part to avoid upsetting this gangster that had suddenly called on his services.

"I've heard a rumor that Haverfords may be contaminating the water supply and that's what is leading to the odd behavior that has impacted Scalestown in such a negative way. Keep in mind, I have absolutely no evidence to back this up. I don't know if it's true. If it is, I don't know if Haverfords is aware or if it's an accident. Like I mentioned, I care about Scalestown. If the decay of our city is because of Haverfords, I want to know," Dustin said.

Dr. Verner looked back with curious interest.

Dustin continued, "I wasn't sure how to get it figured out. I do not want to get Haverfords involved at this stage and risk hurting my relationship if the claims are unsubstantiated. I am quite familiar with your work and thought you could perhaps run tests or lend your expertise to help me try to get to the bottom of this. I must include the disclaimer that this is a highly confidential matter—no one finds out, no matter what."

Dr. Verner did not need telling twice that this was to stay between the three of them. "Thanks for reaching out to me, Daddy Long Tongue. You're quite right—I care about this community and its decline has me quite worried. I've been giving thought to what could be causing the odd behavior amongst our residents but have, so far, been unable to find anything. Your theory could make sense. The water supply would provide a continuous issue for those impacted."

Vladdy interjected, "If it is the water supply, then why isn't everyone experiencing these symptoms?"

"Well, it could be for the same reason that not everyone catches the flu when it's going around. Not all immune systems react the same way," Dr. Verner countered.

"So, you'll look into it?" Dustin asked.

"Yes. I will look into it immediately. I will gather and analyze water samples," Dr. Verner said.

"Excellent, thank you Doctor. When should we expect to hear from you?" Dustin asked.

"Difficult to say. Hopefully next week but one never knows when it comes to science," Dr. Verner replied.

They said their goodbyes and Dr. Verner was off on his way. Dustin was pleased with how the meeting went.

Chapter 67

Volunteers had started coming to Bridgetown to offer assistance. Typically, they brought food and water to hand out. Sometimes they brought blankets or pillows. Jason's favorite was when a group of volunteers would show up with old library books. He enjoyed lying in his bed reading classic novels. These were the same books he would have done everything in his power to avoid reading in high school literature classes. Now, with more time, he wondered why he was so against reading them in high school.

There was a designated area in Bridgetown by the water for lizards to relieve themselves. One morning, Jason had finished doing just that when he saw that there was a group of volunteers handing out books. He rushed over to try to get a copy of something worth reading before they were all handed out. He tapped the woman on the shoulder to get her attention. She turned, and, to his mortification, it was Cassidy. She was there with several other members of the Temple.

She looked surprised. Jason lowered his gaze—he was too humiliated to maintain eye contact with her.

"Jason!" She exclaimed breathlessly as if she had just sprinted several miles. "What are you doing here?"

Jason glanced sideways at his tent. She seemed to piece together that he was not here volunteering but, rather, was a full-time Bridgetown resident.

She lowered her voice to a whisper, "Jason, are you living here?"

Jason sheepishly nodded his head, still avoiding her gaze.

"What happened? I thought you had your own apartment. And you had your job at the donut shop."

Jason shrugged.

"Take a walk with me," she said. She took his hand and started walking towards the designated urination section by the water.

Jason yanked her in the other direction, "You don't want to go down there, trust me. We can go this way."

They walked in silence through the rows of tents until they reached a clearing out of earshot.

"Jason are you ok?" she asked.

"Yeah, I'm fine. It's not as bad as it seems," he lied. "I wasn't happy working so quit my job. I'm here figuring out what I want to do next in life."

"Jason, but living like this? Here? With these people?" she asked cautiously.

He was finally able to meet her eyes. There was a mix of pity and concern. It looked as though she were trying to figure out if this was her fault.

Jason tried to smile, "It's not ideal, but I'm getting by."

"Jason, you can come stay with me for a while if you'd like," Cassidy said. The words came slowly out of her mouth as if she were debating whether she wanted to make the offer even as she was starting to speak it out loud.

Jason would be lying to say part of him didn't want that. But he knew he couldn't. "Thanks, I really appreciate it. But I'm good here. I'm close to figuring things out and will get my own place and land on my feet just fine." He couldn't tell how convincing he sounded.

She nodded her head. They walked back through the rows of tents in silence. She leaned in and gave him a quick peck on the cheek and wished him good luck.

"Cass?" Jason asked.

She turned back around, "Yes?"

"Can I grab a book please."

"Of course."

Jason grabbed a book and thanked her. With that, he crawled into his tent and curled up under a grubby blanket to read.

Chapter 68

Dustin got word from Dr. Verner several days later—the final results were in. The doctor showed up that afternoon to discuss his findings with Dustin and Vladdy.

"Gentlemen. The anonymous tip you received was correct," Dr. Verner said somberly.

Dustin and Vladdy exchanged a look of concern. The doctor then went on to explain his findings, which were quite disturbing indeed. After a thorough explanation, Dustin thanked the Doctor and, again, asked for his discretion until things got sorted out. Dr. Verner thanked Dustin for getting him involved and reassured him that he would keep the findings to himself for the time-being.

After the Doctor left, Dustin and Vladdy sat in silence for several minutes.

"We need to go meet with the leadership team at Haverfords—Douglas, Manuel Jacques and Richard Tarley. Call and set something up immediately," Dustin instructed Vladdy.

"What are we going to say?" Vladdy asked.

"I'm going to tell them what we found out. I'm going to ask them if they knew about it up front. I'm going to tell them the deal is off. That I will not try to protect them from Kerry Bolkanski from running them out of town," Dustin replied.

"You're upset, I get it. But have you thought this through? I don't think we should be making rash decisions based on an emotion we are feeling in the present," Vladdy said.

Vladdy didn't get it. He couldn't care less about Eaglestown. All he cared about was the amount of cash that was rolling in and the lifestyle it was allowing him to lead.

"I have thought it through. I've thought it through quite carefully. I will not let this town seep further into decay while we profit. We've made enough money from the deal as is. And we have other ways money is coming in. This is my town and that fat bastard Douglas Trulio better remember that."

Vladdy stared back at him, containing his frustration. Dustin could tell he was trying his best to hold back from lecturing him about what a dumb decision this was. Dustin maintained his stare without breaking eye contact. A silent message to Vladdy to keep his mouth shut and do what he's told.

Without saying another word, Vladdy reached into his pocket, pulled out his phone, and placed a call to Haverfords headquarters. The incompetent secretary that had been asleep at his desk during their first visit to the Haverfords headquarters answered on the last ring before it would have gone to voicemail. Vladdy stated that he wanted a meeting with Douglas, Manuel and Richard the next morning. He told him it was not possible with their schedules. Dustin took the phone from Vladdy's hand and insisted that the meeting take place and that their schedules be rearranged. It was an emergency, he assured him. His voice was intense and menacing. The aggressive tactic paid off.

The next morning Dustin, Vladdy and Pauric arrived at Haverfords' headquarters. There was much less excitement this time around. The incompetent secretary had indeed managed to get the meeting scheduled correctly. Douglas, Manuel, and Richard were all there waiting for them. Apparently, Dustin's warning at their first meeting that he did not wait for anyone had resonated.

Vladdy entered the room first and shook hands with all three men. Dustin started speaking before they had a chance to shake his.

"As you've no doubt heard, quality of life in Scalestown has been rapidly declining. Unemployment and homelessness rates are through the roof. It's quite concerning. We received a call from a reporter that's on our payroll last week. She said she got a tip that the cause of the issue was Haverfords dumping chemicals into the water supply. The caller had no proof though. I decided to do my due diligence and worked with a doctor and scientist to see if there was any truth to the accusation. The doctor conducted a study and discovered that it is, in fact, the water supply that has been causing the health issues in our town," Dustin said all this quickly. He wanted to get to the point right away before the three Haverfords men could start thinking of excuses.

The three men exchanged confused glances.

"Did you know?" Dustin asked, calmly.

Douglas Trulio was the first to speak. "We have no idea what you're talking about. Nothing about what we're doing is harmful."

"Science disagrees," Dustin replied.

"What science? Do you have a report? We've never run into issues and, quite frankly, this is an offensive, ludicrous claim," Douglas shot back.

"Yes, we have a report. I will be more than happy to share it with you. Maybe you were unaware. But, at the end of the day, it doesn't matter as the damage has been done," Dustin said.

Manuel, usually the quietest of the three, weighed in, "You're out of line. You come into our office and accuse us of causing problems in your community without sharing your proof with us or giving us a chance to speak. You are out of line here, and it is unacceptable."

"You're out of line. What you did to my community is unacceptable," Dustin said, trying to keep his temper under control.

"So, what's this mean?" Richard asked.

"Our partnership is over. There are new members of City Council who will come at you to drive you out of town, and I will not stop them. I'm going to let the newspaper run the article exposing the truth. I'll make sure that it is worded that it was an unknown side effect not a malicious attack on your part. But you will shut this plant down immediately," Dustin said sternly.

"How about we leak that you were the one who sponsored the corruption and profited off of the demise of your suddenly beloved town?" Manuel chimed in.

"How about I kill all three of you? How about I kill your wives? How about I kill your children?" Dustin replied gravely. Of course, he would never harm their families, but they did not need to know that.

"You son of a bitch. How dare you threaten us and our families. You're low-level scum. A thug who thinks you're much more powerful than you really are," Douglas shouted.

Dustin curled his hand into a first and struck Douglas as hard as he could across the face. Douglas let out a howl and collapsed to the floor. Pauric stepped up by his boss's side and flexed his muscles menacingly in case Manuel or Richard was foolish enough to take a step forward. Douglas stared back from the floor, wheezing heavily. Dustin could tell from the look in his eyes that he would never speak the truth and risk facing Dustin's wrath.

Dustin, Pauric, and Vladdy turned and left the office. Their ride back was silent. Dustin instructed Pauric to pull over so he could buy some ice for his aching hand. When they got back, Dustin stepped into the back room and called Beverly. He told her she could run the article but had to phrase it like it was a mistake. She also, obviously, had to leave anything out that could point to Dustin's involvement. She was to say she reached out to Dr. Verner directly after receiving an anonymous tip from a concerned citizen. She could alert Kerry Bolkanski and get quotes from her as well so that City Hall could apply pressure to get

Haverfords booted out of town. He told her he would set up time for her to speak with Dr. Verner. Next, Dustin called Dr. Verner and informed him the *Lizard Daily* would be running a story about Haverfords. Beverly Lowery would be reaching out for an on-the-record explanation of his findings. Dustin instructed him to leave out the part about their conversations and Dustin's involvement. Dustin knew there was some risk that things could be traced back to him, but, at this point, he had made his decision to side with the town he grew up in.

Chapter 69

The article was on the front page of the next morning's edition of the *Lizard Daily*. Mr. Ruggles and Jason read the article at the same time. Mr. Ruggles was in his back office, sitting comfortably in his leather chair with his feet up on the desk. Jason was in the back alley behind the restaurant. He had shown up earlier than usual to try to tap on the back door to get some free donuts from Mathieu. On Jason's walk over, he saw the paper on someone's front steps. The headline was visible, so Jason scooped it up and put it under his jacket as he continued down the street towards Donuts on Blanch. Jason wasn't quite as comfortable as Mr. Ruggles. Instead of a leather chair, he was sitting on a wooden crate. While the conditions the two lizards were reading in differed, the content was the same.

Haverfords' chemicals responsible for Scalestown's Demise

By Beverly Lowery

Kerry Bolkanski pulled off a major upset when she ousted incumbent City Counselor, Casper Fitzpatrick. She became incredibly popular with the average Scalestown resident who was concerned about the downward trajectory of our town. Afterall, unemployment and homelessness are at an all-time high and attendance rate in schools and places of worship are at an all-time low. A major piece of Kerry's platform was to increase taxes on big businesses and even attempt to vanquish out-of-town conglomerates that she deemed were taking advantage of everyday residents.

Well, it turns out she was right. Last week, I got an anonymous tip that chemicals in our water supply caused by Haverfords were causing people to act strangely and leading to the uncharacteristic behavior patterns in Scalestown. So, I did what any investigative journalist would do and started looking into it.

I turned to medical expert Dr. Arthur Verner for help. For those who don't know, Dr. Verner is a highly respected doctor and scientist who has been involved with several major medical discoveries. Dr. Verner took samples of the water supply and analyzed them carefully.

"I can without a doubt say that our water supply has been tainted by chemicals coming from Haverfords and that it has directly impacted the health of our community," Dr. Verner told me. When I asked him to elaborate, he said:

"The chemicals in the water interact with the brain to produce harmful side effects. It causes lizards to become numb to their normal feelings. It slows their brainwaves so that they lose energy, motivation, concentration and the will to participate in normal day-to-day activities. This is, most likely, directly causing the increase in unemployment and homelessness. It's also, most likely, causing the decline in school attendance. Lizards aren't functioning at a high percentage and it's impacting their lives negatively. While not a malicious attack by Haverfords on our community, it's something we haven't seen before. We need to be careful with how we deal with the situation. The chemicals have an addictive component."

Addiction, according to Dr. Verner, is a theory that has only recently started to be explored by lizards in the medical community. Essentially, it is the inability to stop consuming a chemical even though its causing harm to the brain or body. This is why Dr. Verner is preaching caution and continued research and the need for close collaboration with local government. There could be 'withdrawal' effects that impacted lizards could experience, causing sickness.

I reached out to Kelly Bolkanski for comment. "This proves what we've long suspected—outside big business having a negative impact on our community. I'd like to thank the Lizard Daily and Dr. Verner for investigating to uncover the truth. We will work very closely with medical experts to make sure we come up with a solution that is the safest for our town. The City

Council looks forward to making positive changes to return Scalestown to its glory, and I look forward to leading the charge."

The Lizard Daily will continue to update the fine residents of Scalestown with any and all pertinent information.

Mr. Ruggles put down the paper, surprised that Dustin had gone through with shutting down Haverfords. Jason put down the paper, surprised to find out the problems he was experiencing may not be entirely his fault. It was a lot to take in.

Chapter 70

A few days later, Jason was playing cards with Artie in his tent while munching on a donut. Nothing had changed yet. He, and all his fellow Bridgetown residents, still felt and acted the same way. It would take time, Jason told himself, for the town to figure out how best to solve the problem.

Artie was winning. Jason was strategizing his next move when he heard his name being called in the distance. He recognized the voice but couldn't quite place it. Artie heard it as well. "Mathieu" Jason said out loud.

"Who's Mathieu?" Artie asked.

"The chef from Donuts on Blanch. What the hell is he doing down here?"

"I'll have to thank him for all the free donuts," Artie said grinning.

Jason popped his head out of the tent and saw Mathieu a few paces away peeking into random tents while calling out his name.

"Mathieu!" Jason shouted out. "Over here!" He waved him over to the tent.

Mathieu looked relieved to have found him. "Can we talk?" Mathieu asked, glancing around at the other lizards. This was clearly his first time over here.

"Sure, come on into my humble abode," Jason said jokingly.

Mathieu stepped into his tent. Jason introduced him to Artie.

"I was hoping we could speak in private," Mathieu said awkwardly, diverting his gaze to avoid eye contact with Artie.

"It's all good Mathieu, Artie is a good friend. What are you doing down here?" Jason asked.

"I think it's the donuts," Mathieu blurted out.

"You think what's the donuts?" Jason asked.

"That's causing all the problems." Mathieu looked over his shoulders and around the filthy tent. "All of this."

Jason looked back at him, confused. "What are you talking about, man?"

"I think there's something in the donuts that's causing people to act funny," Mathieu replied.

"Didn't you see the article in the paper the other day? It was big news. It's the water supply that's causing the issues. That big company Haverfords is responsible," Jason said wondering how Mathieu could have missed hearing about that.

"I read the article, yes," Mathieu said. He continued slowly, "But I don't believe it. Well, I believe the premise of it, but I don't think it's the water supply that's causing it. I think it's the donuts."

Jason looked back at Mathieu like he was crazy. "Why do you think that?"

"This Dr. Verner guy. The one who found the chemicals or whatever. Over the past few weeks, he's come into Donuts on Blanch multiple times and met with Mr. Ruggles in the back office. Each time Mr. Ruggles has asked not to be disturbed while he goes in with him."

Jason stayed silent and waited for Mathieu to continue.

"I didn't think much of it until the day after the article came out. It was later in the afternoon and Mr. Ruggles had stepped out. There was an issue with the cash register and the back up one was in his office. I'm the only one with a spare key, so I went in to grab it. On his desk, I saw a check made out to Dr. Arthur Verner for $25,000," Mathieu said.

Jason stayed silent for another minute. It was odd, but he was skeptical. "How do you know what the money was for?"

"Well, I don't know for sure. But just think about it, Jason. Look around. The people down here by the bridge...think of how many are regulars at Donuts on Blanch. I saw a dozen in this stretch of tents alone. They were regulars when we first opened. They were furious when we stopped selling the original recipe. As soon as we got the original recipe back, they started coming back every day. Even now, living in tents with barely enough food to eat, they spend their only pennies coming up to Donuts on Blanch each day," Mathieu said.

Jason didn't reply. He was trying to absorb the information. Could there be truth to this? Now that Mathieu mentioned it, the majority of people he saw down here had been regulars. And he knew Mathieu was right about many of them going to Donuts on Blanch every day. It was like a great migration each and every morning.

Mathieu continued, "Even think about yourself Jason. You ate those donuts every single day. Practically for every meal. When the original recipe went away, you got filled with anger. That's when you went to jail, that's when you seemed frustrated every minute of every day. There was anger throughout the entire town at that time. Hell, you even got attacked by someone demanding an original donut! Even though you knew the donuts sucked, you still tried them every day just in case. And then the original recipe came back, and you started gobbling them down again for just about every meal. It must have caught up to you. Think about it, Jason. Now you match all the symptoms they are talking about with the water supply. You lost interest in work. You lost energy, motivation, the ability to concentrate...literally everything that article outlined. You stopped showing up for work. You didn't care when you got fired. You got kicked out of your apartment and have been living in a freaking tent!"

Jason glanced over at Artie. He looked shocked. Jason guessed his face mirrored Artie's expression. A realization set in. "Holy shit. Mathieu. That makes a scary amount of sense."

Mathieu smiled shyly. Despite it being bad news, he looked relieved that he wasn't being ridiculed for sharing it.

"So," Jason asked, "What do we do about it?"

"I think we have to go talk to Dr. Verner about it. See if we can get him to admit it's the donuts and not the water supply. I took a picture of the check and have it on my phone. I think it's our only shot," Mathieu said.

Artie hadn't said a word since Mathieu entered the tent but suddenly chimed in, "I can help with that."

"You can?" Jason asked. "What do you mean?"

"Dr. Verner is my dad. I'm Arthur Verner Jr.," Artie replied.

Jason was caught off guard. Here he had made this new, great friend yet he was only now realizing he hadn't even known his last name or where he came from.

"I haven't talked to him in a while. He doesn't know I'm living down here. If it's true, we need to get him to admit it so these people can go back to their normal lives," Artie said.

"And so we can burn down Donuts on Blanch," Mathieu said quietly. He looked as though he was struggling with guilt. He had been, after all, the one who had prepared these donuts.

"Meet me at my house tonight. We can be there waiting for him when he gets back from work," Artie said.

After a brief silence, Jason got Artie to open up about why he was living under the bridge when his father was a successful doctor with a home a few miles away. Artie told him that, while his father was from Scalestown originally, he had moved out west to pursue his education. While out there he and Artie's mother, Chloe, met but did not know each other very well when Artie was born. They got separated soon after, but both remained in his life. Artie would split his time between the two of them. His father worked long hours and traveled often for work, so Artie saw much less of him. While it sounded like his mother had her issues (perhaps she wasn't ready to have a child), he developed a closer bond with her. When he was 10, she packed up and left the town without much of an explanation. Artie moved in with his father full time. The only reason his dad has stayed in the area was so that Artie could have a relationship with his mother. Now that she had run off, his dad thought it best if the two of them moved to Scalestown. It was tough leaving his friends as a ten-year old, as well as moving in full time with a man he hadn't spent a ton of time with. Over the next few years, Artie grew to like Scalestown and his relationship with his dad grew. When he was sixteen, his mother reappeared and reached back out. She apologized for leaving and told him she had done some soul searching and wanted to be his mother again. She wanted him to move back in with her. Artie's dad thought it was a bad idea. Artie was doing well in Scalestown, and he didn't trust Chloe to be a dependable enough parent for their son. Artie couldn't quite articulate to Jason why he decided to move back with his mother. Was it that he missed her? Did he need a mother? Or, was he hurt she left and wanted to prove her wrong that he, in fact, was worth sticking around for? Either way, much to his father's dismay, Artie packed his things and moved back west to live with his mom. Artie and his dad would speak on the phone, but, over time, those calls grew less and less frequent as his relationship with his father dwindled. A few years went by and Artie was happy. He made friends, got himself a girlfriend and graduated high school. Then one day, for no real reason, his mother packed up her things and left again. Artie stayed in the area and went to college. He went on to get a good job and continued to date his high school sweetheart. His job was demanding, though. Artie found himself working too many hours, just like his father had done. This ended up leading to the deterioration of his relationship with his girlfriend. After the two of them broke up, Artie decided to go visit his father in Scalestown. The visit went well, and Artie decided he wanted to move back. He held back from telling his father about his decision in case he changed his mind. Artie was staying at a motel in Scalestown while he started to look for work, but most places weren't hiring. He couldn't find work, started eating a strict diet of donuts from Donuts on Blanch, and, gradually, his money ran out. He was too embarrassed to show up at his dad's in his current state so, like many other Scalestown lizards, ended up living in a tent down by the bridge.

A few hours later, they got in Mathieu's car. Artie gave directions from the back seat. It would have been a far walk, so Jason was thankful they were getting a ride. They hadn't talked through the plan exactly. It seemed like Artie would lead the way and they'd wing the rest.

Mathieu parked a few mailboxes down. The three of them went and sat on Artie's front steps, waiting anxiously. It was quite the impressive house—not a complete shocker for a well-known, successful doctor.

Artie stood up as he recognized his father's car coming up the long driveway. He looked uncomfortable. Dr. Verner exited his car cautiously. He appeared to be squinting trying to tell who the people were on his front steps. Jason saw the look of realization creep onto his face.

"Artie?" Dr. Verner asked sounding surprised. "Is that you?"

Chapter 71

Mr. Ruggles was sitting at home, happy and relaxed. His phone rang. The volume of his ringtone was set too high and it caught him off guard. It wasn't a number he recognized, but he answered anyways.

"Hello?"

"Mr. Ruggles?"

"Yes," Mr. Ruggles replied.

"It's Amir Kalil."

Mr. Ruggles knew Amir Kalil quite well. He worked at the *Lizard Daily*, and they often exchanged favors. Amir would publish favorable articles that helped Mr. Ruggles' interests as well as give him helpful tips sometimes. Mr. Ruggles made sure to take care of Amir with free tickets to sporting events and gift cards to his favorite restaurants. It was like having a less powerful Beverly Lowery. Amir did not have nearly the following Beverly did. You could normally find his articles buried three or four pages into the paper. Often, his pieces weren't covering the sexiest of topics. Nonetheless, a good contact for Mr. Ruggles to have in his rolodex.

"Hi Amir—how are you?" Mr. Ruggles asked.

"I'm well, Mr. Ruggles. I just got a very interesting phone call. Well, I should say we just got a very interesting phone call," Amir replied.

"Oh? What kind of phone call?" Mr. Ruggles asked.

"Well, first off, just to double check...I'm a big fan of 'The Sun Kissed Brothers'...and I hear they will be coming to Scalestown next month. What are the chances you could get tickets?" Amir asked.

Mr. Ruggles rolled his eyes. The Sun Kissed Brothers was some lousy band. Mr. Ruggles was familiar with a song or two but didn't listen to garbage like that. He preferred the classics. "Depending on what type of call we're talking about, I'm sure I could acquire some tickets."

"I just got off the phone with two lizards who claim to work at Donuts on Blanch. They did not give their names. They want the paper to investigate an issue," Amir said. He was enjoying drawing out the conversation.

"What issue?" Mr. Ruggles asked.

"They're claiming it's Donuts on Blanch that is causing the health problems in Scalestown. Not Haverfords," Amir said.

Mr. Ruggles heart skipped a beat. He had thought he was in the clear. How did they figure it out? Who was it? There's no way—he had been so careful. No one had suspected a thing.

"What?" Mr. Ruggles tried to sound innocent. "What did they say exactly?"

Amir continued, "They claim they saw a check for a large sum of money made out to Dr. Verner. They then said they paid Dr. Verner a visit and got him to admit he lied about Haverfords. That it was actually Donuts on Blanch that caused the issue. They said Dr. Verner is willing to go on the record. This could be a big story—and a big break in my career."

Mr. Ruggles paused. There was no point in trying to play innocent. He needed to be direct and to the point. "Amir, I will pay you $10,000 to listen to me very carefully and do just as I say. I'll also throw in those concert tickets—front row."

"I'm listening," Amir said.

"Call the two lizards back. Tell them in order to run the story, you need a copy of the check receipt they saw on my desk. If you don't have that, it won't be enough to go off. Tell them to meet you at Donuts on Blanch at 9pm. Do not actually show up. Do not ever speak a word of this to anyone," Mr. Ruggles said while trying to remain calm.

Amir said, "How about we make it $15,000?"

"Fine, $15,000 it is," Mr. Ruggles replied. Amir could ask for just about any sum of money right now and Mr. Ruggles would agree to it. How could he not?

"Ok, I'll make the call. Always a pleasure, Mr. Ruggles," Amir said.

"Amir—one more thing. At the beginning of this conversation I think you used the word 'we' got an interesting phone call. Was there another person in the room for the call?" Mr. Ruggles asked.

"Yes," Amir said. "Beverly Lowery."

Shit.

"Give her a call and tell her you found out it was a bogus claim. A hoax someone was playing on you. Something like that," Mr. Ruggles said.

"Sure thing, Mr. Ruggles."

Mr. Ruggles thanked him and hung up the phone. He was really in trouble now. Beverly would surely rush off to tell Dustin about the call.

Mr. Ruggles had planned it from the very beginning. He knew the Glaze Haze product was "addicting" (as it was now being called per Dr. Verner). When he first talked to Karim about being partners, Karim explained that lizards would keep coming back for more. They'd be "hooked" as Karim put it. Once they tasted it, their bodies would need it and they would have no choice but to keep coming back and spending money. Mr. Ruggles couldn't have predicted the wide-spread destruction it would cause, but he'd be lying if he said he wasn't aware it would be harmful to the lizards of Scalestown. When they lost the ability to use Glaze Haze,

Mr. Ruggles knew he'd lose customers. It was also Mr. Ruggles who made the anonymous call to Kerry Bolkanski tipping her off about Haverfords leaking chemicals into the water supply. Once she won her City Council seat, he knew he had to focus her attention elsewhere if he wanted to stay successful. What better target than the out of town conglomerate she rallied against during her campaign? He had, of course, fabricated the entire story that Haverfords was to blame. Mr. Ruggles guessed that Dustin would be conflicted about the harm his partnership was doing to the community and would be willing to end it if it could be proven the rumors were true. Although a gangster, Dustin was still genuinely a good, caring lizard at heart. That bet paid off big time. Mr. Ruggles had already plotted with Dr. Verner on lying about the results of the Haverfords test. Although a successful doctor, he had made some reckless financial decisions over the past few years and needed the money. Mr. Ruggles was unsure how he would get Dr. Verner the opportunity to do the testing, so he was elated when Dustin reached out proactively to him seeking his advice. Dustin confessed to him that he wanted to do the right thing, so all Mr. Ruggles had to do was make that subtle suggestion of using the doctor to investigate. Dr. Verner played his role perfectly. He easily convinced Dustin that Haverfords was to blame and even matched the symptoms the town was experiencing from the donuts to the chemicals in the water. As predicted, Dustin parted ways with Haverfords—the good in him outweighing the gangster. Mr. Ruggles could imagine how infuriated Vladdy must be with that decision. He also got satisfaction thinking about Douglas Trulio, and the smug look he had on his face when they first met, being run out of town. Better still, Dustin gave Beverly the 'ok' to publish the article and quote both Dr. Verner and Kerry Bolkanski. This all but guaranteed that eyes would be exclusively on Haverfords and that Mr. Ruggles could continue making an enormous amount of money at Donuts on Blanch undisturbed.

But now things had changed completely. He had tricked the politicians, the press, and the most powerful gangster Scalestown has ever seen...yet somehow two of his employees had put it together. He needed to act. He took out his phone and called Karim.

Chapter 72

J ason's mind was racing. Mathieu had been right. He was playing the scene over in his head still trying to comprehend it. Dr. Verner had walked up the stairs and, upon recognizing his son, hurried forward and gave him a hug. It was a somewhat awkward embrace—one between two lizards who at one time were close but couldn't remember when that was.

Artie introduced Jason and Mathieu. Dr. Verner then invited them inside. The inside of the house was just as beautiful as the outside. Expensive looking art hung from the walls and a giant golden chandelier dangled down from the ceiling. Dr. Verner had offered the group food and drinks, which they declined. After exchanging some small talk, Dr. Verner asked his son where he had been.

"Well, Dad," Artie began, "I've been living down by the bridge."

Dr. Verner looked shocked. "The bridge? In the community of pop-up tents?"

"Yes," Artie said, looking quite embarrassed.

"What were you doing down there?" his father asked. It was then that Dr. Verner started taking stock of his son and of Jason. The dirty clothes, the stench, the grime and mud—all of it.

"I didn't plan to be. Things had been going very well for me," Artie began. "But then I started feeling differently. I lost all energy. I was nervous all the time and couldn't concentrate. I stopped looking for work, caring about my appearance, caring about my life. I didn't know what happened to me, and I, quite frankly, didn't care enough to find out. My friend, Jason, here experienced the exact same thing," Artie had said, motioning to his left in Jason's direction. He continued, "Then the other day I saw your article. Well, the article you were quoted in I should say. Things started to make more sense."

Artie then paused to try to get a read on his father's reaction. Dr. Verner's body drooped slightly. His eyes had filled up with a look of guilt. He didn't say a word.

"Then Mathieu showed up today. He works at Donuts on Blanch. Have you been over there, Dad?" Artie had asked.

The Doctor nodded.

Artie continued, "He said he found a check receipt with your name on it for $25,000. He also made some good points about who is suffering down by the bridge—regulars at Donuts on Blanch."

The Doctor was now looking down at his lap.

"I know we haven't always seen eye-to-eye, Dad. But lizards are struggling. Lizards are dying out there. Lizards are living in filth and squalor. Me being one of them. My friend, Jason, being another. I need to know; did you lie about the Haverfords study? Are the donuts what's really causing the problems?" Artie asked.

Thinking back, this was the most awkward moment of the encounter with Dr. Verner. Jason had always been uncomfortable with grown male lizards crying or showing much emotion in general. Probably because his father wasn't in touch with his emotions and viewed crying as a sign of weakness. Artie's dad, at that point, lost it. Jason could tell he had been trying to hold off tears, but once they started, the floodgates opened, and he wept like a baby lizard hatching out of the egg. It had taken him what felt like forever to gain his composure enough to speak.

"I'm sorry, Artie," he said. "And I'm sorry to you as well, Jason. Yes, I did lie about the Haverfords test results. Mr. Ruggles paid me to lie. He paid me a large sum of money. I didn't ask questions. I don't know if the donuts are actually what's causing it or not."

Artie had looked at his father skeptically. He was a smart enough doctor to put the pieces together.

Dr. Verner looked even more embarrassed now that he had tried to play it off like he didn't know it was the donuts. He had said, "Ok, yes I'm sure it's the donuts. I'm sorry, I shouldn't have gone along with it."

"Sir." It was Mathieu, normally shy and quiet, who interjected. "You need to tell the truth. You need to go on the record so that Donuts on Blanch can be shut down and this community can start to heal."

Dr. Verner sniffed in hard. "I don't know, I don't know," he said desperately. "The man I lied to is dangerous. I could be killed."

Jason realized it was Daddy Long Tongue that Dr. Verner had tricked. He shuddered thinking back to his experience with Pauric and didn't blame the doctor for fearing repercussions.

Artie had shot a hard stare at his father. "Dad. Many more lives will be ruined."

Dr. Verner's tears started flowing again. His whole body had been shaking. When he had composed himself enough to speak, he agreed to go on the record with the truth.

After that, Jason and Mathieu left Artie at home with his dad. They called the *Lizard Daily* to tell them they had a big story—they wanted to speak to the woman who had done the initial report on Haverfords. Surely, she would be interested in this story and do a good job with it. A man named Amir answered the phone instead. They asked to speak with Beverly Lowery. He said she wasn't available. In the background, they heard her holler out that she was available. There was some muffled talking and it sounded like Amir and Beverly had reached an agreement that they would both run with the story together. Jason and Mathieu filled the two reporters in—that Dr. Verner was willing to go on the record to be quoted. Amir thanked them for their time and said they would return their call shortly. They purposely did not leave their names—Jason wasn't sure where Daddy Long Tongue fit into the equation. He knew Pauric collected that money every week on Daddy Long Tongue's behalf. The gangster may not be pleased if Donuts on Blanch got shut down and that weekly money stopped coming.

Jason was snapped back into the present by the vibration of his phone in his pocket. He looked down and it was the same number at the *Lizard Daily* he and Mathieu had dialed. Amir.

"Hello?" Jason asked.

"Hello, fellas. It's Amir. I did some digging around on my end. It sounds like it could be a big story and that you two could be heroes. To publish it, I need a copy of the check receipt that you saw in the office though. While Dr. Verner's quotes will be powerful, the physical evidence will make it much stronger and leave little room for doubt."

"Just to be clear," Jason began, "we're not looking to become heroes. We'd like to remain anonymous."

"Of course, of course," Amir said. "Can you meet me at Donuts on Blanch at 9pm? You can head in and get the copy and give it to me. I should be able to hit the deadline to get the article into tomorrow's paper if I am able to get those quotes from Dr. Verner tonight as well. It will be a late night for me—but well worth it!"

Jason glanced at Mathieu. He continued, "We'll get the copy. Like I said though, we want to remain anonymous so handing it to you directly would defeat that. There's a bench about 25 yards down Blanch Street. We will leave it in an envelope for you."

"That works. Keep an eye out for tomorrow's paper," Amir said before hanging up his phone.

Chapter 73

Karim picked Mr. Ruggles up. It was another car Mr. Ruggles did not recognize. Amir had called moments earlier letting him know that the two employees, still anonymous, would be meeting at Donuts on Blanch at 9pm to head inside to get a copy of the receipt. Karim and Mr. Ruggles had a couple of important stops to make before that 9pm meeting.

Mr. Ruggles rushed outside and scurried into Karim's passenger seat. Without taking a breath, he launched into the story to bring Karim up-to-speed.

"Ok," Karim said. "So, we need to shut the two kids up as well as make sure word doesn't get back to Daddy Long Tongue."

"He may already know," Mr. Ruggles replied. "Beverly may have gone straight to him. She is the immediate threat. Dr. Verner won't go to Daddy Long Tongue proactively, but I can't see him putting up much of a resistance to an interrogation from Pauric."

"Neither can I," Karim said in agreement.

"First stop, let's swing by her office and see if she's still there," Mr. Ruggles said.

Karim nodded and started driving towards the *Lizard Daily*'s building. On the way, Mr. Ruggles called Amir to see if he spoke with Beverly. He assured him that he had. He told her it was a guy he had gotten in an argument with a few weeks back trying to pull a fast one on him. Mr. Ruggles pressed him trying to figure out if she had believed him. Amir claimed that she did. She hadn't left the office or made any phone calls since they spoke. This gave Mr. Ruggles and Karim the slightest bit of relief.

They pulled onto a street behind the parking lot of the building.

"How long do you think she stays at the office?" Karim asked.

"I don't know. Probably depends if she's trying to hit a deadline or not," Mr. Ruggles said.

The two men waited in silence. It was now 7:30 pm, and there was still no sign of Beverly. They had several other stops they needed to make, not to mention getting over to Donuts on Blanch to be set up before these two anonymous employees stopped by. Mr. Ruggles suspected it was Mathieu. He observed more than he let on.

"I think we need to call her," Karim said, breaking the silence for the first time in what felt like hours.

"And say what?" Mr. Ruggles asked.

"I don't know. You're supposed to be the clever one, Mr. Ruggles. Something to lure her out of the office?" Karim replied.

Mr. Ruggles pulled out his phone and dialed the main number for the newspaper. He asked to be transferred to Beverly Lowery.

"Beverly Lowery, *Lizard Daily*," she said in a professional voice.

Mr. Ruggles tried his best to mask his voice by speaking a few octaves lower than normal. "I have a hot tip for you on the Haverfords story. We need to meet immediately. I have a train leaving town in 20 minutes. Meet me in the parking lot of the train station."

There was a pause on the other end, "What's the tip?" she asked.

"We'll talk in person. Will you come meet me there now?" Mr. Ruggles asked in his fake accent. He wasn't sure how well he was pulling this off. He had never called in a fake news tip before, nor did he sit at home practicing fake accents.

"How will I find you?" Beverly asked. Her tone made it sound like she had plenty of experience meeting up with anonymous callers in random places.

"I'm standing by the ticket counter in a blue jacket, ball cap and wide-framed glasses," Mr. Ruggles said and hung up the phone.

Karim started laughing. "Mr. Ruggles, you sly bastard, that was beautiful."

Mr. Ruggles smiled—he was quite proud of himself for that performance. He pointed, "She'll take a left at the end of the road down here. About two miles further, there are no streetlights and very little traffic."

"Perfect. Good thinking with the train station. Quick on your feet, aren't you my friend?" Karim replied. "Here switch seats with me."

"Why?" Mr. Ruggles asked.

"Because I can't drive and do the dirty work," Karim said in a serious tone.

The two lizards got out of the car. Mr. Ruggles got into the driver's side and adjusted the seat. Karim piled into the passenger's seat, sitting down with such force the entire car rocked.

"Is that her?" Karim asked.

"Yes, I think it is," Mr. Ruggles replied. Adrenaline was starting to kick in.

"Ok, have you ever tailed anyone before?" Karim asked.

Mr. Ruggles gave him a look indicating that he had not.

"No worries. Just listen to me, my friend, and we will be perfectly fine. The key is to stay back far enough that she doesn't notice you. You know where she is going so you can slow down until she turns first before going around a corner yourself. When we get to that stretch in two miles, you'll accelerate and get right on her ass."

Mr. Ruggles nodded as he put the car into drive. Beverly had just started her ignition and was now backing out of her parking spot. Mr. Ruggles waited until she was out of the lot before moving his car.

"Good, good. Just like this, my friend," Karim encouraged him.

One more turn and they'd be on the poorly lit, open stretch of road. Mr. Ruggles realized he wasn't sure what the "dirty work" was that Karim planned on doing while the car was still moving.

They made the turn.

"Ok, step on the gas," Karim said as though he were coaching a teenager behind the wheel for the first time.

Mr. Ruggles pressed his foot down and accelerated.

"Good. Now really step on it. Get as close as you can. Flip on your high beam lights so she can't see in her rearview," Karim told him.

Mr. Ruggles sped up even more. He was practically on top of Beverly's car. He could tell she was checking them out in her mirror. He flipped on the high beams to disrupt visibility. Beverly started increasing speed to escape the tailgating and the harrowing glow of the lights. Mr. Ruggles kept pace.

Karim tried rolling his window down but couldn't. He tried a second time—still nothing.

"Shit," Karim said. "The child locks must be on or something. Turn them off!" he yelled at Mr. Ruggles.

Mr. Ruggles looked around frantically. He had never driven this car before. He had no idea where the child locks were. His eyes darted back and forth until he found the lock symbol. He pressed it and heard the click of Karim's window being unlocked.

"Come on, speed up!" Karim shouted.

Mr. Ruggles brought his eyes back to the road. While he was distracted looking for the child lock button, Beverly had pulled ahead. Mr. Ruggles knew that this dark stretch ended in another half mile. They needed to act quickly. He stepped on the gas and caught back up to her bumper. Karim rolled down the window and brandished a gun from his belt. He leaned his head and right arm out the window and started pulling on the trigger relentlessly. Bullets bounced off the back of Beverly's car. One smashed through the back windshield; glass flying everywhere, including the hood of their car. Karim fired again. Mr. Ruggles could see Beverly's shoulder drop. She lost control of the wheel and the car began spiraling. It skidded without slowing speed and smashed into a tree on the side of the road. Mr. Ruggles swerved to avoid a collision. He slammed on the breaks. Karim was reaching for the door handle when there was a massive explosion. Beverly's car was engulfed in flames. Karim stopped reaching for the handle and signaled to Mr. Ruggles to get the hell out of there.

Mr. Ruggles guided the car towards Dr. Verner's house. Dr. Verner had betrayed them and, therefore, couldn't be trusted. They didn't want to call him in advance and spook him. Mr. Ruggles knew he lived alone and figured it best to drop by unannounced. They parked a few mailboxes away. Karim reached into the glove compartment and refilled his gun with fresh ammunition. He also retrieved a thin looking tube that he attached to the end of the gun.

"It's a silencer," Karim explained. "Makes it so the gun shots aren't as loud."

"We need to find out who else he told. If anyone," Mr. Ruggles said.

The two men exited the car and walked up the driveway to the house.

"Not too shabby," Karim said under his breath.

Mr. Ruggles knocked on the door. Karim reached up and extended his gloved finger over the peephole so that the Doctor would not be able to tell who it was at the door. They could hear footsteps shuffling towards them. It wasn't Dr. Verner who opened the door, though. It was a younger lizard whose features looked very similar to the doctor's. Could be his son, Mr. Ruggles thought to himself.

There was an immediate look of recognition on the lizard's face as he made eye contact with Mr. Ruggles. He tried to slam the door, but Karim was too quick. Karim wedged his knee in between the door and the wall to stop it from shutting, lowered his shoulder, and, like a battering ram, forced himself through the threshold of the home. The younger lizard flew backwards and landed on his back.

"Artie?" It was Dr. Verner's voice from the other room. He peaked his head around the corner and saw Karim's gun pointed at his son. His face went white.

"Dr. Verner," Mr. Ruggles said. "Good evening."

Dr. Verner didn't even attempt to lie. "Look. This is my son. He has nothing to do with our business. Let him go. Please."

"Who else knows?" Mr. Ruggles asked as calmly as possible. He needed to find out. He must find out.

"Let the boy go, and I will tell you anything you'd like," Dr. Verner said, his voice shaking.

"The boy stays. Now answer the question," Mr. Ruggles said.

"If I answer, will you let him go? He won't say anything. He lives far away from here. He'll pack up and leave tonight and won't say a word to anyone." Dr. Verner mentioned nothing of saving his own life. He must have already concluded that it was forfeit.

"Yes, we can do that," Mr. Ruggles replied. There was no way they could do that.

Dr. Verner avoided looking at Artie. He took a deep breath, "Two younger lizards came here earlier. They had proof that we lied about Haverfords. Artie and I have been here since then. We haven't spoken to anyone."

Mr. Ruggles believed him. "What were their names?"

Dr. Verner paused, concentrating. Trying to pull the names from his brain. Knowing that this information, perhaps, could keep his son alive. "One of them was Mathieu."

Mr. Ruggles' suspicions were confirmed. It was too bad; he liked Mathieu. The thought of harming him was quite distressing.

"What about the other?"

"The other. What was the other's?" Dr. Verner said. Pleading with his memory. "Artie what was the other lizard's name?"

Artie remained silent.

"Damn it, Artie. Tell them," Dr. Verner pleaded.

Karim raised the gun and pointed it at Artie.

"It was Jason!" Dr. Verner screamed triumphantly. "Jason was the other lizard's name."

Upon hearing his friend's name, Artie lunged towards Karim. He did not move nearly fast enough. Karim put a bullet in him before he had even fully left the ground. His body went limp, and a pool of blood started to form on the tile floors.

Dr. Verner looked down in shock. "Do it."

Karim obeyed his command and pulled the trigger. The doctor slumped over. They were both dead.

Karim and Mr. Ruggles ran back to the car. Mr. Ruggles thought he was going to be sick. Multiple people were dead tonight. And, while he didn't pull the trigger himself, the blood was on his hands just as much as it was on Karim's.

What pained him the most was the thought of hurting Jason. Even with Jason's erratic behavior, caused by the donuts most likely, Mr. Ruggles cared for him like a son. Well, not like a son. But he cared. And that was rare for Mr. Ruggles. He wasn't going to kill either of them, he decided. He'd threaten them with Pauric. Jason would remember all too well what Pauric's firsts were capable of. He'd stuff a large amount of money in their pockets and tell them to flee from Seglestown and never come back. There had already been enough death tonight.

Chapter 74

Dustin was sitting at his table playing cards with Vladdy, Pauric, and another lizard who would occasionally join them. In the movies, the head gangster typically took everyone's money, but Dustin was a novice and lost more often than not. The game was interrupted by frantic knocking at the door.

Dustin exchanged suspicious glances with Pauric and Vladdy. Pauric pulled a gun out of his waistband. Dustin walked over to the window and peeked out. It appeared to be a woman. And she appeared to be injured. Dustin waved to Pauric that he could put the gun down and opened the door. It was Beverly Lowery.

She was hardly recognizable. Her face was covered in blood and mud. A car was backing down the driveway. Beverly took a step forward before collapsing on the floor. Luckily, Dustin was able to stop her from hitting her head, but the rest of her body wasn't as lucky. She let out a groan of pain. She was panting as if out of breath.

Dustin called Pauric and Vladdy over. The three of them lifted her up and placed her on the couch. She was bleeding heavily and, from the color on her face, she had lost a lot of blood already. Dustin's first thought was for her safety, his second thought was that he'd need a new couch. He chastised himself for letting a thought like that even enter his mind.

"Beverly, Are you ok? What the hell happened to you?" Dustin asked. "Pauric, get some rags and water. We need to stop the bleeding." Pauric leapt into action to find the necessary items.

"Who was that in the car?" Vladdy chimed in.

Beverly attempted to shrug but winced in pain. "I don't know. He was driving by the wreck and stopped. I asked him for a ride."

"What wreck? Why did you come here—why not a hospital? You need to get to a hospital," Dustin said.

"Because I needed to tell you something. I don't know if I'd be safe at a hospital," Beverly replied weakly.

Vladdy pulled the other lizard, who was there to play cards, off to the side and asked him to wait in the back room while they talked with Beverly.

"What do you need to tell me?" Dustin asked. Was this girl going to die on his couch?

"I was in the office earlier today. My co-worker and I got a call. It was from two lizards that claimed they had proof that Haverfords wasn't causing the health issues. They said that it was being caused by Donuts on Blanch," Beverly took a deep breath. It was taxing for her to speak.

Dustin and Vladdy were hanging on every word.

"They said they saw a check-receipt from Mr. Ruggles to Dr. Arthur Verner for a large sum of money the day after my story was published. They claimed they had gone and talked to Dr. Verner and convinced him to admit that he lied about Haverfords and was paid off by Mr. Ruggles to do so. My colleague was skeptical. He said there was a lizard who had been messing with him by trying to get him to publish phony articles. I guess the guy had been misquoted and wanted to get back at him. So, my colleague, Amir, made a few calls to dig into it. A few minutes later he came into my office and said he figured out it was that guy just making the whole thing up," Beverly explained to them.

The room remained silent.

"So, I didn't think twice about it and believed him. This sort of thing happens every now and then. Then, this evening, I got a call from someone saying they had a tip for me. Again, pretty typical. The guy said he was leaving on a train and to come meet him in the parking lot of the station. I agreed." She was struggling to get through her words now.

"Beverly?" Dustin said as gently as he could. "Then what happened?"

Her eyes opened back up. "I left the office and was driving over there when this car started tailgating me. I just thought it was some asshole. But then they started shooting at my car. With a gun. I think I got shot in the shoulder. Either that or it was a big shard of glass. Either way, I lost control of the car and went spinning into a tree. I hit the tree hard. There was glass everywhere and my head was ringing. All I knew was that I wanted to get out of that car. Away from the smoke and broken glass. I crawled over the seat and rolled out of the car. Another second later it exploded. I don't know how I didn't get killed."

Could this be true?

"Another car drove by a few minutes later and saw the wreckage. I think it was a few minutes. I don't know. He picked me up and offered to drive me to a hospital, but I had him drop me here instead," Beverly said.

Dustin turned to Pauric. He motioned towards the back room, "Have him drive her to the hospital right now. Have him pay any expenses and we will reimburse him later." Pauric nodded and went to retrieve the other card-player.

"It must have been Mr. Ruggles. He must have gotten tipped off about the report," Vladdy said anxiously.

The pieces started fitting together. Mr. Ruggles wanted to use Glaze Haze so badly. He sold so much of it because it was addictive. It was Mr. Ruggles who recommended that Dustin use a third-party to evaluate the water. It was even Mr. Ruggles who suggested using Dr. Arthur Verner, Dustin realized.

"Who was the other reporter?" Dustin asked, trying to remain calm. "Beverly?"

"Amir Kalil. He lives close by," she replied. "His number and address are in my phone."

Dustin reached out and grabbed her purse to get her phone. How she had managed to remember to grab her purse through all that was beyond him.

He searched for his name and it pulled up. She was right, his address was probably ten minutes away.

"He usually texts me back very quickly. I think he has a little thing for me," Beverly said, trying her best to smile.

"Beverly, you're going to get a ride to the hospital. This gentleman right here will stay with you to make sure you're safe while you're there. Take care of yourself. I'll come visit and drop your phone off later. Thanks for coming to us with this," Dustin said earnestly.

He started typing out a text to Amir on Beverly's phone but turned it over to Vladdy instead.

"Hey"

"Hi Bev. What's up?"

"I'm in your neighborhood. Are you home? Thought I could swing by."

"I'm home. I'll just have to put something on first ;)."

"Ha-ha, ok sounds good. See you soon."

Poor bastard, Dustin thought. Seeing Pauric enter his house instead of Beverly would be quite the letdown. Hopefully, he does put something on.

Dustin, Vladdy, and Pauric went out to the car. They needed to find out if Amir knew the truth, and if he knew where Mr. Ruggles was now. It was 8:30pm.

Chapter 75

"Do you think you can trust this other reporter?" Karim asked Mr. Ruggles.

"Amir? I trust his greed. He won't talk as long as he's taken care of," Mr. Ruggles replied.

"Well, we don't have time now. But perhaps we will pay him a visit later, just to be sure," Karim answered.

"Yes, we can do that. I don't care what happens with him," Mr. Ruggles said.

They pulled up to Donuts on Blanch. They wanted to get there early to get in position before Mathieu and Jason showed up.

Mr. Ruggles paused, trying to think of the best way to phrase the message he wanted to communicate. "I don't want the boys harmed, Karim."

"What boys? These boys? Coming here? What are you talking about?" Karim asked.

"Yes. Jason and Mathieu. They are both good kids and worked hard for me. We can threaten them and then pay them to leave town and then let them know if they come back, they're dead. Neither of them has family, homes, or girlfriends here. Hell, one of them is homeless."

Karim didn't answer right away.

"Trust me," Mr. Ruggles continued, "Jason had to deal with Pauric. Pauric beat him bloody for no reason. He isn't going to want to deal with something like that again. And, he stayed loyal. He never told anyone about what happened that day. And it allowed our business to flourish."

Karim broke into a smile, "Ok, my friend. We're going to have to toughen you up, eh? You're a softie! But, yes, no problem. If you trust them; I trust them."

Mr. Ruggles nodded in approval. They walked up to the entrance of Donuts on Blanch and went inside. Mr. Ruggles kept the lights off and they settled into a booth, patiently waiting for the arrival of their prey.

Chapter 76

Pauric reached out his massive firsts to pound on the door of Amir's house. Dustin held his hand up to stop him, though. Instead of pounding loudly, Dustin tapped the door gently, emulating the sound Beverly's hand might make. He covered the peephole with his thumb so that Amir would not be able to see out.

Amir opened the door in a bathrobe with a wide smile on his face. The smile turned to confusion. He looked at them, one after the other. He paused on Pauric and glanced him up and down, the sheer size impressing him, as it did most lizards. This certainly wasn't Beverly Lowery.

"Can I help you?" he asked.

Per usual, Pauric's hands moved lightning fast. He punched Amir square in the chest. Amir fell backwards, opening the pathway into the home for Dustin and Vladdy. Amir slowly got to his feet.

"What the hell?" he wheezed. "I think you have the wrong apartment. Who are you? What do you want?"

"You received a call from two lizards claiming they had evidence that it wasn't Haverfords causing the problems in Scalestown, but, rather, the donuts being served at Donuts on Blanch. Is that correct?" Dustin asked.

Amir was looking around at the three of them wild-eyed. He didn't reply. Pauric picked up a lamp that was sitting on a table and smashed it next to Amir's head. The bulb shattered on impact and glass littered the hardwood floor. It got his attention.

"Yes, I did, that's correct," he said, speaking rapidly.

"Did you alert Mr. Ruggles of this phone call? And did he, in turn, bribe you to keep it quiet?" Dustin asked calmly.

Amir looked shocked that they knew. He didn't answer right away. This time a chair smashed over his knee. Pauric smiled down at him as if implying that any time he didn't answer a question, something else in his apartment would get crushed on top of him.

"Yes, yes, yes," Amir said. He was speaking very quickly now. "He offered me money to tell Beverly Lowery that it was a hoax tip and to tell the two callers that, in order to publish the story, I would need them to bring me the receipt of payment from Mr. Ruggles to Dr. Verner."

Dustin didn't even need to ask his final follow up question. Amir blurted out the answer unprompted.

"I told them I would meet them at Donuts on Blanch at 9pm tonight. Mr. Ruggles said not to show up."

Pauric delivered a kick to the same knee he had smashed the chair on and then flipped over Amir's kitchen table for good measure. "Keep your mouth shut or I'll be back."

Mr. Ruggles, you son of a bitch, Dustin thought. He had underestimated the evil that dwelled within his former mentor. It must have been Mr. Ruggles who blew up the Haverfords plant. At the time, Dustin didn't think he was capable of that type of destruction. But he clearly was. The fact that he let the town decay the way it had was despicable. Mr. Ruggles had Dustin convinced with his speech about caring for Scalestown because they were locals. Because Scalestown had been there for them through times of trouble.

Dustin glanced at his watch—it was 8.45pm. Time to head to Donuts on Blanch.

Chapter 77

Jason was nervous. He was following Mathieu up the sidewalk to Donuts on Blanch. Yes, they had a key to the front door, but they were still, in a sense, breaking in. Jason remembered seeing the police officers happily accept Mr. Ruggles' bribe the night he bailed him out of jail. How sympathetic would these police officers be if they showed up and saw Mathieu and Jason sneaking around the property? This was a dangerous situation. Sadly, Jason's other thought was around stuffing a handful of donuts into his pockets on the way out the door. The more he thought about it, this addiction stuff must really be a thing. His mind devoted any spare seconds it had to fantasizing about his next donut.

Jason had to admit, he was impressed with Mathieu. He never pegged him as a hero leading a crusade to help save the town. Mathieu was going out of his way to fix a problem that wasn't impacting him directly. Not to mention it would put him out of a job. Jason tried to warn Mathieu about the dangers of Daddy Long Tongue and Pauric to make sure he understood what he was getting himself into. Mathieu said he understood. Jason doubted he could completely understand since he had not been on the receiving end of Pauric's massive claws pounding him into oblivion.

The two young lizards approached the front door. Mathieu pulled the key out of his pocket and inserted it into the lock. Jason glanced over his shoulders nervously, but the street looked quiet. They crept inside Donuts on Blanch. The store was cloaked in darkness. Jason didn't need to see to know where he was—

the familiar smells flooded his nose and triggered his memories of taking orders behind the counter.

Jason and Mathieu had talked over strategy earlier. They debated just turning on the lights but decided they didn't want to draw any attention. Mathieu had a couple of flashlights lying around in his basement, so they'd use those instead. They slithered over towards the back office, each moving as quietly as they could. Jason could hear Mathieu's breathing and assumed Mathieu could hear his. As they got to the door, Mathieu began fiddling with the keys trying to identify which belonged to the office. Jason held his flashlight steady on the lock so that Mathieu could operate effectively. Out of the corner of his eye, Jason thought he saw the slightest movement.

Chapter 78

As instructed, Pauric was driving towards Donuts on Blanch. Dustin was sitting next to him. Vladdy was in the backseat deep in thought. The three of them were trying to figure out how they had been duped so badly. Dustin was embarrassed. Not only was he tricked by Mr. Ruggles, he also canceled the Haverfords deal. He was hurt that Mr. Ruggles would do this to him. Sure, they had their disagreements, and Dustin wasn't supportive of Donuts on Blanch, but this still felt wrong. Over the past few months, Dustin had been trying to leave his life of crime behind him. He was volunteering and donating money. He was showing compassion where he might not have always done so in the past. He would definitely be closing down Donuts on Blanch, that much was for sure. What to do with Mr. Ruggles though? He kept asking it over and over in his mind. Dustin knew he should shoot him. If word got out that a lizard could trick and take advantage of Daddy Long Tongue without any repercussions, he'd be finished. What if he just took all of Mr. Ruggles' money and sent him packing? Would that be enough? Afterall, Mr. Ruggles had helped him growing up. Dustin's other concern was Vladdy. If Dustin didn't retaliate against Mr. Ruggles, would Vladdy see it as a sign of weakness and be tempted to try to run Scalestown himself? They were a few blocks away, so Dustin had some serious thinking to do in a short amount of time.

A sound came from the back seat. Vladdy had cleared his throat as if preparing to speak.

"Boss?" Vladdy said.

Dustin turned over his shoulder. Vladdy was seated behind him so it was difficult to speak with him face-to-face.

"Yes, Vladdy?" Dustin replied.

"Do you think it's the best move to shut down Donuts on Blanch?"

"What do you mean?" Dustin asked.

"Well, we already lost the money coming from Haverfords. I highly doubt we could save that relationship even if Beverly published an article with Dr. Verner admitting that he lied and that it was actually Donuts on Blanch. That new politician, Kerry Bolkanski, is too headstrong to bring Haverfords back. Not to mention, Haverfords probably wouldn't want to work with us anyways after our..." Vladdy did not finish his sentence.

"After our what, Vladdy?" Dustin asked, although he already knew Vladdy was referencing his mistake in dealing with the Haverfords situation.

Vladdy seemed to be weighing his words carefully.

"Miscalculation. After the miscalculation of what happened. The decision, the meeting with them, everything," Vladdy said.

Dustin sighed, "Yes, Haverfords won't work out in the future, I agree. And yes, I misplayed that meeting and the whole ordeal with them. I take full responsibility for how everything played out. But we're closing Donuts on Blanch down, Vladdy. It's destroying this town. And we can't let Mr. Ruggles get away with it."

"Oh, I agree—Mr. Ruggles can't get away with it. But only a few people know about the donuts, and we can take care of that. Why not kill Mr. Ruggles and take over the business ourselves? He was cleaning up on that place. We can keep the relationship with Glaze Haze and just continue as usual. Work with that buffoon ourselves—Karim or whatever his name was."

Dustin remained silent in the front seat.

Chapter 79

Mr. Ruggles flipped the light switch on. Jason and Mathieu stopped in their tracks and jumped around in surprise. They had thought they were alone. Mr. Ruggles and Karim had shown up a few minutes before and were seated at a booth facing the office. They waited for the two lizards to get far enough from the exit that they wouldn't be able to make a run for it.

"Good evening boys. Do you come in here after hours often?" Mr. Ruggles asked.

Neither Jason nor Mathieu responded. Karim stood next to Mr. Ruggles; his gun drawn for intimidation purposes. It was working. A dark stain formed on the front of Mathieu's pants. It appeared as though he had lost bladder control and wet himself.

"Which one of you figured it out first? Mathieu, I assume it was you since you were still working here?" Mr. Ruggles asked.

Mathieu gave Jason a look out of the corner of his eye before nodding to Mr. Ruggles.

"Don't worry, boys. We aren't going to hurt you. In fact, I will pay you right now under two conditions," Mr. Ruggles said. "Would you like to hear them?"

Both boys nodded back at him, indicating that yes, indeed, they did want to hear the two conditions that could keep them alive.

"First, you never speak a word of this to anyone. Second, you leave Scalestown immediately. No going home to pack things up, no farewells to friends or family. I mean, straight from this store, you will leave town and never return."

Jason and Mathieu looked at each other in confusion trying to process what the catch was.

"If you do mention this to anyone or if you do return to Scalestown for any purpose at any time, there will be trouble," Mr. Ruggles said.

Still silence.

"Jason, do you remember when you met Pauric for the first time?" Mr. Ruggles asked.

Jason nodded, yes. He looked beyond uncomfortable.

"Well, this would be much worse. Instead of Pauric's firsts, you'd be looking straight down the barrel of a gun. Do I make myself clear?" Mr. Ruggles asked. He sounded as if he were lecturing an elementary school class.

Before either boy could answer, there was a loud bang accompanied by a scream. Mathieu dropped to the floor. Mr. Ruggles stood stunned, his ears ringing. He turned his head and saw Karim standing with his gun drawn. He had shot Mathieu square in the chest.

"Karim, what the hell!" Mr. Ruggles screamed, "I told you, I didn't want them hurt."

"We don't have time for this shit, Ruggles. I don't trust them. I'm not putting everything at risk hoping they keep their stupid mouths shut," Karim said back.

Karim then turned and pointed the gun at Jason with the intent of repeating the cruel act that just took the chef's life. Jason stood frozen.

Something inside Mr. Ruggles roared to life. Seeing Mathieu's lifeless body, and the look of pure terror on Jason's face caused him to snap. Karim disrespecting his commands was almost as infuriating. Mr. Ruggles lunged at Karim and knocked him backwards, just as Karim was about to fire a shot at Jason. Karim seemed stunned that Mr. Ruggles had tackled him. Mr. Ruggles was, perhaps, more stunned that he had done it. The element of surprise gave Mr. Ruggles an advantage. He was in the process of getting Karim pinned to the floor as they grappled over the gun. Karim outweighed him by at least forty pounds. He was also a younger lizard than Mr. Ruggles. He regained his balance and drove Mr. Ruggles backwards. Now both lizards were furiously fighting to get control of the gun.

Chapter 80

Pauric pulled the car into an open parking spot outside of Donuts on Blanch. Dustin unbuckled his seatbelt as he prepared to exit the car to confront his former mentor. The three lizards heard a gunshot come from inside the building. They weren't the first to arrive.

Then, Dustin felt it. A cold metal pressed firmly against the back of his head.

Vladdy pulled the trigger from the backseat; blood painted the car. And, with that, the reign of the most powerful gangster in Scalestown history had ended. Dustin had shown weakness, and Vladdy capitalized on it.

Chapter 81

Jason looked on in disbelief. Mr. Ruggles and this other lizard were in a battle for the gun and a shot went off. At first, Jason couldn't tell who had been hit. A moment later he recognized the voice that was letting out a string of profanities that would make Marvin Deholmes at the Temple blush. It was Mr. Ruggles who'd been shot. He clung on to the other lizard for dear life. The other lizard pushed him aside as he struggled to catch his breath. Mr. Ruggles collapsed and was bleeding profusely from the stomach screaming in agony. Jason froze. To his left lay Mathieu, dead. Directly in front of him lay Mr. Ruggles, most certainly moments away from death himself. As disgusted with Mr. Ruggles as he was, his last act had been to try to save Jason's life. The other lizard was fighting to get back up on his feet, using a toppled over chair to gain the necessary leverage to be able to stand.

The back door sprung open. In rushed Vladdy and Pauric, guns drawn. Pauric had his gun aimed at Karim. Karim's was aimed back at Pauric. Vladdy noticed that Mr. Ruggles and Mathieu were both laying lifeless, so he pointed his gun at Jason. Jason threw his hands up into the air as quickly as he could to indicate he was unarmed. Upon seeing that, Vladdy pointed his gun back at Karim.

"Drop the gun, Karim," Vladdy said. He tried to remain calm, but this was not his area of expertise.

"I'll drop my gun when that ugly giant drops his," Karim said, nodding at Pauric.

Pauric stared Karim down, his finger itching to pull the trigger.

"Pauric, lower your gun," Vladdy said slowly.

Pauric wasn't as quick to respond to an order from Vladdy. Maybe it was because he hadn't adjusted to Vladdy being the boss yet, or maybe it was that Dustin knew what he was doing in situations like this and Vladdy was an amateur.

"Pauric," Vladdy repeated. "Lower your gun."

Pauric, begrudgingly, lowered his gun. Vladdy kept his pointed at Karim.

"Thank you," Vladdy said. "Now, Karim. Lower yours."

Karim lowered his arm. Vladdy seemed to be gaining his confidence that he was handling the situation well. His first test as head gangster.

Vladdy lowered his arm as well. "We know it's Donuts on Blanch that caused the addiction problems, not Haverfords. We know that Dr. Verner lied to Daddy Long Tongue. Beverly Lowery managed to escape your attack. She came to us and filled us in. We went to the other reporter, Amir's, house to verify her version."

Karim nodded, impressed that Beverly had made it out of that car crash alive. "The doctor's dead. His son too. We paid him a visit earlier. So, he won't be able to verify any of this."

Oh no—Jason thought. Artie's dead.

It was Vladdy's turn to nod; impressed that they had already gotten to Dr. Verner. "What happened here with Mr. Ruggles?"

"These are the two kids that figured out it was Donuts on Blanch causing the addiction," Karim said. "Ruggles didn't want to hurt them. He wanted to pay them to leave and never come back. I didn't want to leave something like that to chance so shot that one," Vladdy pointed at Mathieu's corpse. "Ruggles attacked me and the gun went off in the struggle."

Jason made eye contact with Pauric. It seemed to have just dawned on Pauric who he was. He started grinning and blew Jason a kiss.

"Ah, the cashier," Vladdy said, nodding in Jason's direction.

"Where's your boss?" Karim asked.

"Outside in the car with a bullet in his brain," Vladdy said.

Karim looked back and forth between Vladdy and Pauric, "Who pulled the trigger?"

"I did," Vladdy replied.

"Had to prove you were capable of something like that?" Karim asked.

"Something like that." Vladdy continued, "Pauric and I talked about it at length first. We both felt it was necessary. Daddy Long Tongue got tricked and lost us the money on Haverfords. Then his plan was to come down here and stop this profitable operation. He has a soft spot for Scalestown. And a soft spot for Mr. Ruggles. I tried reasoning with him and telling him that we couldn't afford to lose out on this money now that we had lost Haverfords. Why not kill Mr. Ruggles and continue operating Donuts on Blanch as usual? He disagreed. So, I put a bullet through the back of his head."

Karim nodded with a curious look on his face—no doubt wondering what would happen next.

"What do you think? Should we partner up and keep this operation up and running?" Vladdy asked.

Karim smiled. "Absolutely. We were making great money."

Karim tucked his gun in his belt and walked across the room to shake Vladdy's hand.

"Pauric, will you take our friend, the cashier, out back and dispose of him? I'd like to review some of Mr. Ruggles' financial records. I'll call someone to come down here to help clean up this mess," Vladdy said.

Pauric smiled. It was a creepy, genuine smile. It didn't seem like anything could give him more pleasure than getting to dispose of Jason to end his night.

"Come on over, sweetheart," Pauric called over mockingly.

Jason started walking across the room towards Pauric. He debated trying to run out the other door but knew he would never make it. He tried to avoid looking at Mathieu's body but couldn't help it. He tried to avoid looking at Mr. Ruggles' body but couldn't help that either. Pauric opened the back door and extended his arm as if ushering him to his seat at a theater show.

Chapter 82

Pauric was leading him around the back of the building into the alley with a dumpster. Jason could feel the piece of glass in his left hand. It was warm from how sweaty his palms were. During the confusion of Vladdy and Karim's standoff, Jason was able to bend over without being noticed and pick up a shard of glass from a broken vase. The shard was a little longer than Jason's hand. If Pauric looked directly at him, he'd be able to tell it was there. So far, Pauric's eyes had not lingered in that direction, and, under cover of darkness, the piece of glass remained undetected. The glass was sharp, but Pauric's scales were thick and Jason wondered whether the monster was even capable of feeling pain.

Jason had no plans of going down without a fight. Had it not been for Mathieu being killed, he would have willingly followed Pauric out the door, climbed into the dumpster on his own accord, and warmly welcomed the bullet as a permanent guest into his brain. Mathieu was innocent, though. He was a good lizard who risked everything to try to help his town, expecting nothing in return.

They were almost at the dumpster. Pauric, who was walking behind him, gave him a nudge with the tip of his gun to keep him moving in that direction.

"Climb on in," Pauric said.

Jason knew it was time to act. Now or never. He dropped unsteadily to his knees and started making sounds and head movements as though he was throwing up. The darkness hid the fact that, despite the theatrical sounds, no liquids were coming out. Pauric reached down to pick him up to toss him into the dumpster himself. He felt Pauric's hand start to graze his back. Jason turned and thrashed his arm around as violently as he could. The glass grazed the right side of Pauric's face before plunging into the left side, landing in his eye.

Pauric recoiled and screamed. The scream started as surprise and quickly changed tones to reflect anger and sheer madness. Pauric dropped his gun in an effort to use both hands to pry the shard of glass from his left eye socket. Jason leapt towards the gun. Pauric must have sensed his movement. He swung wildly in Jason's direction. The punch was thrown too high in the air. Jason picked up the gun. He realized he had never held one, let alone fired one. Was the safety on or off? Pauric managed to yank the glass out of his eye. He turned and saw Jason starting to raise his own gun towards him.

Pauric was charging at him. Jason raised the gun and fired. The first shot sailed to the right of Pauric and clanged into the dumpster behind him. How could he miss at this range? Pauric was now a few steps away from striking range. Jason adjusted his aim so he wouldn't miss to the right and pulled the trigger. The next shot hit Pauric in the left shoulder. Pauric's body dipped in that direction and he let out a grunt of pain, but it didn't stop his charge. The next shot hit him in the stomach. The next in the thigh. The shot that caused him to drop to the ground hit him higher in the chest. The shot that caused him to stop wriggling on the ground hit him right in the head. Jason fired more shots at the motionless body until there was a clicking sound letting Jason know he had no more bullets left in the gun.

Another shot rang out and clanked off the dumpster. Vladdy and Karim must have heard the commotion and come outside to investigate. Jason now wished he hadn't wasted the rest of the bullets on Pauric's motionless body. Then again, was he really going to win a shoot-out against these two?

Luckily, Jason was thin. There was a small gap behind the dumpster that connected to the adjacent alley way. Jason used to sneak through it to knock on the backdoor to ask Mathieu for his daily supply of free donuts. More shots were fired but Jason slipped through the gap unscathed. He ran as fast as he could. His legs pumped as hard as they could. He couldn't remember the last time he had run like this. After fifty yards he was out of breath. A diet of addictive donuts combined with a lethargic lifestyle were not good for stamina. Jason looked over his shoulders and realized he was not being followed and slowed his pace. Vladdy and Karim did not know Scalestown. They probably couldn't see the small passage that connected to the other alley. Either that or they couldn't fit through it. There's no way Karim could, the chubby son of a bitch. Jason doubled over and actually threw up this time.

Chapter 83

Now what? Jason knew he needed to flee Scalestown. It was far too dangerous to stay. He headed back towards the bridge. He had a few dollars in his pocket but had also buried some money under his tent. The money had come from selling his free donuts second hand to his desperate neighbors. It should be enough for a one-way train ticket and a couple of nights in a hotel when he got to his new destination while he figured out what he'd do next. He was thirsty. And hungry too.

To an outsider, trying to find your way to a specific tent in Bridgetown would be a near impossible task. Jason navigated the maze of tents in the darkness like an expert though. Take a left at the purple tent with the white polka dots, veer right past the four large garbage cans that always had a fire burning inside—a beacon to guide Jason on his walk home—and, finally, turn left at the large rock that usually had wet clothes drying on it.

Jason entered his tent and lifted a piece of tarp he had put over the top of the hole to keep it covered. He reached for the tiny spade-shovel he had borrowed from Artie. Karim's voice popped into his head telling Vladdy he had already killed Dr. Verner and his son. He had yet to process his friend's death, let alone grieve for it. But he needed to escape Scalestown first. He carved the spade into the ground and dug up a clump of dirt to retrieve his money. There were a few more dollars there than he recalled. Jason packed up the rest of his belongings in his old high school backpack. There wasn't too much to pack. As he exited his tent, he reasoned he might as well take a look into Artie's possessions as well. Jason ducked in even though he knew time was of the essence. He grabbed a flashlight, pair of socks, and a winter hat and stuffed them into his bag. He saw a picture of Artie with an old girlfriend and tucked that gently into his bag as well.

He exited the tent and started his walk towards the train station. There was an older man sitting on the ground outside of a tent eating a donut. Jason noticed he had a full box sitting next to him. Dr. Verner may have been lying about what was causing the addiction, but he hadn't been lying about the concept of addiction itself. Jason longed for one of the donuts. The thought of leaving them behind may be scarier than the thought of Karim and Vladdy tracking him down. He noticed how hungry he was. Perhaps it was best to take one last donut for the road. Jason stopped and asked the lizard if he could have one. The lizard looked back at Jason like he had to be kidding. Jason rolled his eyes and started digging into his bag to find his money while asking the lizard how much one would cost. The lizard demanded a price well above market-value. Jason countered and offered him half of what he asked. The lizard nodded his head and smiled, accepting the money while extending the box for Jason to take his pick of the litter. It was a tough decision, but he ended up choosing a *Scalestown Breeze*—a raised brioche donut filled with fresh strawberry cream, topped with pineapple glaze, candied lemon, and topped off with a raspberry drizzle.

The *Scalestown Breeze* was a work of art. Jason plucked the donut out of the box with extreme care to preserve its beauty. He pulled his bag off his back to put his wallet back in and set it down to keep the donut protected. As he shifted the contents in his bag to make room for his wallet, the picture of Artie was staring back at him. Deep down, Jason knew that if he took a bite of that donut, he'd use the rest of his money to buy the lizard's entire box. The euphoria of eating multiple donuts would cause him to sit back down in his tent without a care in the world. From there, who knows if he'd ever get up.

Jason hoisted his bag back up on his shoulder. Before he could change his mind, he handed the donut back to the lizard he bought it from. The lizard looked confused and started to tell him there were no refunds. Without asking for one, Jason walked straight past him, made his way through the rows of makeshift tents, and headed towards the train station without looking back.

Made in the USA
Middletown, DE
24 July 2021